Bernice Rubens was born in Wales and later read English at the University of Wales, of which she is now a Fellow.

Her writing career began when she was thirty and around the same time she started work in the film industry. For some time, Bernice alternated between writing novels and making films. For the last ten years she has concentrated solely on writing. Her novels to date include the Booker Prize Winner *The Elected Member* and *Five Year Sentence* which was shortlisted for the Booker Prize. In 1987, Bernice was on the Booker Prize jury and she has also won the Welsh City Council Prize for *Our Father*. Two of her books have been successfully transferred to film; *I Sent A Letter To My Love* and most recently *Madame Sousatzka*, directed by John Schlesinger and starring Shirley Maclaine. *Kingdom Come* is her latest novel.

Bernice's other love, apart from writing, is playing the cello. She has two daughters.

*Also by Bernice Rubens in Abacus:*

BIRDS OF PASSAGE
BROTHERS
THE ELECTED MEMBER
A FIVE YEAR SENTENCE
I SENT A LETTER TO MY LOVE
MADAME SOUSATZKA
MR WAKEFIELD'S CRUSADE
OUR FATHER
THE PONSONBY POST
SET ON EDGE
SPRING SONATA
SUNDAY BEST
GO TELL THE LEMMING
KINGDOM COME

# MATE IN THREE

*Bernice Rubens*

AN ABACUS BOOK

First published in Great Britain by Eyre & Spottiswoode (Publishers) Ltd 1966
Published by Hamish Hamilton Ltd 1987
Published in Abacus by Sphere Books Ltd 1989
Reprinted 1991
Copyright © Bernice Rubens 1966

ISBN 0 349 10104 3
Printed and bound in England by Clays Ltd, St Ives plc

Sphere Books Ltd
A Division of
Macdonald & Co (Publishers) Ltd
165 Great Dover Street, London SE1 4YA
A member of Maxwell Macmillan Publishing Corporation

*For my mother*

PART ONE

As they turned into Upshot Rise where his parents lived, Jack let go of Ruth's hand. Upshot Rise was not a hand-holding street. When you turned into it, you wiped your feet and minded your manners. Each house was decently detached, each privet hedge crew-cut and correct. Each drive sported a car or two, and the portals of most of the houses were framed by white pillars that had probably been delivered in polythene bags. Behind each set of white curtains lived people who touched each other seldom. Some had retired and moved into the suburb for the landscape and the silences. Whilst others had begun there, sprouting from the white sheets in the white beds behind the white curtains, who knew nothing of dirt except that of conception and delivery.

Jack's parents fitted neither of these categories. They were German refugees. Not the mattress-on-the-donkey-cart type of refugee, winding in tracking-shot down the interminable highway, but respectable well-heeled emigrants. The flight of the Müllers had been in the early days, without panic and with all their possessions. Jack's father's business had been an export affair to England so that there was little upheaval in their change of address. Both his father and his mother spoke English fluently, and through the business were already well connected with the upper strata of English social life. They travelled first class from Ostend to Dover, and early in the morning when only the white cliffs were looking, they dropped the umlaut on their name, and landing as the Millar family, they spoke to the customs officer in faultless English, declaring their monogrammed silver. Upshot Rise was a natural home for them. It was almost a duplicate of the Beethovenstrasse where they had lived in Hamburg. Quiet, silent, and reliable. Like Upshot Rise, it lay in a dream suburb, a suburb of dream houses, a spotlessly clean nightmare.

Jack and Ruth walked unjoined up the hill, and turned into the house that took in the bend of the road. Jack tried to silence the click of the gate as he opened it to let Ruth through. He knew that his mother would be waiting for the noise behind the bedroom window. It was the first time she would see Ruth and Jack wanted to give her no time advantage. He wanted them to meet at the door and see each other at the same time. He hesitated before ringing the bell. He noticed that Ruth was trembling. Somehow he couldn't put her at her ease. She had cause to be nervous. His parents wouldn't approve of her. He began to regret that he'd brought her there at all. He could have married her and told them afterwards. Yet he couldn't help himself. He had to bring her. It was as if he needed a declaration of their hostility before he could possibly marry her.

He put his hand on her arm and smiled reassuringly. She was small, so small she hardly reached his shoulder. He took a small comb out of his pocket and gave it to her. She shrugged her shoulders and made a gesture of putting it through her thick black hair. It broke in two in the process and she threw the pieces irreverently on to the front lawn. No. His parents wouldn't like her at all. Her blouse was embroidered and low-cut, tucked into a wide peasant skirt.

That ensemble wouldn't go down well either, despite the stockings that he had insisted she wore, and the white gloves, that in his mother's eyes were the hallmark of elegance. She had drawn a line at carrying a handbag, and his pockets were stuffed with her diary, his/her handkerchief, and her conker, which for some reason, she carried about with her everywhere. In her nervousness she drew the gloves off her hands. Her finger-nails were still clean, but alas, Jack wondered, for how long. In the course of the afternoon, from nowhere the dirt would come, and lodge at home beneath the nails. By tea-time, she would have abandoned her shoes, alien to her forever-sandalled feet, the slide on top of her hair would relinquish its unaccustomed hold, and her hair would fall free to her shoulders, the front locks creeping behind the embroidery of her blouse. By the time tea was over, she would have reverted to the exact picture that he had first caught sight of in the café, a few months ago, a pulsating almost ugly, ungroomable waif, whom he had loved on sight and without reason. She smiled at him as a signal that she was ready for the fray. When she smiled her whole face co-operated, her black eyes crinkled, and her long thin nose puckered at the bridge. He became aware of how Jewish she looked. Undeniably. His parents would hate her. He felt like a boxing promoter, launching a new discovery against impossible odds. He nodded at her and rang the bell.

A uniformed maid opened the door. She had been with the Millars since their arrival in England some years ago. She still wore the uniform embroidered with the family initial that the Müller servants had worn in Germany.

"Hullo, Millie."

"Master Jack," she said. "It's nice to see you again."

"This is Ruth," he said, pushing her forward.

Millie nodded with a formal smile. She had obviously been rehearsed by his parents.

"They're in the sun-room," she said, leading them through the house.

Jack was a little annoyed that his parents hadn't opened the door, that they had been sitting all the time unconcerned at the back of the house. But it did not surprise him. There was a sense of cool ceremony about his parents, that sometimes, especially since he had met Ruth, deeply offended him. Whenever there was an emotional crisis in the family circle, whether of joy or sorrow, it was celebrated decently, coldly, and with every formality. He had the feeling that if his father suddenly died, his mother would stretch across to the phone by the deathbed and make immediate and highly efficient arrangements with the undertaker.

Ruth was not grateful for the reprieve. She wanted to get the meeting over with. She lagged behind Jack as he walked into the sun-room. His parents looked round as he came in. Mrs Millar took one eyeful of her threatened daughter-in-law, and resumed her knitting. Mr Millar just stared at Ruth open-mouthed.

"This is Ruth," Jack said feebly. Mr Millar nodded and Jack motioned her to sit down. There was an interminable silence, broken only by the rhythmic click of Mrs Millar's needles.

"You have a lovely garden," Ruth heard herself saying. Mr Millar had partially recovered from the initial shock of his son's choice.

"Later on, I'll show you round," he said. "It takes two gardeners three times a week to keep it in order."

Mrs Millar looked up from her knitting.

"My wife does a little of course," he added hastily. "She plans it all."

"You do a wonderful job, Mrs Millar," Ruth said.

Mrs Millar muttered under her breath. Praise from such a quarter as Ruth's was not to be taken seriously. What did she know of landscape gardening anyway? She looked as if she had spent her whole life in a caravan.

"How's teaching?" Mr Millar asked. "Have you had a raise yet? You're smoking too much. Do you smoke?" He pointed his chin at Ruth reluctant to address her by name.

"Yes," she admitted.

"You're not going to be much good to my son in that respect then, are you?" He smiled, fearing that he had been too harsh with her. "You see," he leaned forward, "he can't afford it on his salary."

He talked across Jack as if he weren't there.

"I've begged him to come into the business, but he wants time for his writing, so he has to take a teaching job for next to nothing a week. I don't mind him writing," he said generously, "but it should be a hobby. Like I play the violin. For pleasure."

"But he's a serious writer." Ruth was horrified at the ease with which he diminished his son.

"What kind of living can you make from poetry?" his father dribbled on. "What kind of society can he mix in? Bohemians, that's all. Beards and pipes and dirty clothes. It's not for him," he confided. "He's been used to better things."

Ruth wanted to go away. Jack had warned her of his parents' attitude. She had a sudden fear that he too would become infected by their standards, that when they married and had children, he would impose on them his father's wishes which he himself was unable to fulfil. She looked at Mrs Millar and hated her. Though she said nothing, Ruth felt that Mr Millar was talking for his wife, silently prompted, as she had probably prompted him all their married life. With her knitting needles, she had conducted the tempo of his living, his work and his leisure. He could live only at her suggestion.

Suddenly Mrs Millar put down her knitting and stared at Ruth.

"What does your father do?" she said with a distinct lack of optimism in her voice.

"Does it matter?" Ruth said indignantly.

Jack touched her arm. She had promised to co-operate. Yet here, after only five minutes she was already opting out of the game. He began to dislike her a little. He looked down at her feet and was not surprised to find that one shoe was easing off her foot.

"Tell her," Jack almost commanded.

"He's a tailor."

"Oh."

"My mother works too," Ruth donated gratis. She was beginning to enjoy the shocks they were suffering. "She helps my father. He plays the violin too," Ruth went on.

Even this piece of information could not arouse Mr Millar's interest. They both looked with dismay at their son, wondering how such a calamity had befallen him.

"Show Ruth the garden," Jack said.

He wanted to talk to his mother alone. He wanted to sell Ruth to her. Secretly he wanted her approval, so that he wouldn't have to marry her.

Mr Millar got up and motioned Ruth to accompany him. She made a gallant effort to reshod herself, but on second thoughts stepped out of both shoes, and trotted stock-inged-feet alongside an astonished Mr Millar.

When they were out of ear-shot, Mrs Millar put down her knitting.

"And where did you find that?" she asked.

"Her name's Ruth."

"She looks like a gypsy."

"What's wrong with that?"

"Jack," Mrs Millar said patiently, "when you were a child in Germany, you mixed in the best social circles. When we came here we sent you to a good school, a good university. It was not without some sacrifice on your father's part. You met people of good account, you had entrée through your father's connections to the aristocracy of this country. And what did you do to repay us for all this? You left a good home, and took God knows what kind of room in London. You refuse to go into the business and you do a job which pays you nothing. And to cap everything, you pick up this girl, and you have sufficient disrespect for your family to bring her here and expect me to entertain her. I have said all I want to say."

"I'm going to marry her," Jack said. His mother would never understand how skilfully she had talked him into it.

"You'll do it on your own," she said. "Now that she's here, I shall give her tea. After today, I don't want to see her again."

In a way, Jack was relieved. If his mother had accepted Ruth, he would have regarded it as a token of rejection of himself. By accepting his choice of partner, his mother diminished him. The prospect of a friendship between them deeply disturbed him. Yet when he married he would need her as a background of tension, an outpost of permanent and reliable hostility. He loved his mother against all reason, and for a moment he sensed Ruth as an intruder.

He looked across the lawn and saw his father walking between the rose-gardens. Ruth was lagging behind him, smelling each colour. Her nails by now were probably filthy.

His father looked sad, but Jack was not moved by his melancholy. He felt himself only remotely connected with his father. It was his mother who claimed his sole attachment and she would have to die before he could consider his father as his sire. Yet he was grateful to him that at least he had made some kind of effort to contact Ruth. At least he had been polite. He watched him walk towards the terrace into the lengthening shadows of his mother's knitting, and momentarily he pitied him. He swore to himself that he would never allow Ruth to tyrannize him. His mother's tyranny had made his father weak and contemptible.

They moved silently into the dining-room where tea was laid. Ruth had put on her shoes, but the over-full slide on her hair had finally capitulated. As she sat down, it fell on to her bread and butter plate and white napkin. Mrs Millar clenched her teeth and turned away. Jack noticed her reaction and he stood behind Ruth's chair. He gathered the two side pieces of hair, and tugged them cruelly into the slide. He needed to punish her for his mother's sake. Then he sat down by her side. She stretched out her hands on the table. Ten black half-moons on the white cloth.

"And what are you going to do about these?" she asked him.

She folded her hands in her lap. She had made her point. He looked at her. The prospect of such exciting incompatability almost frightened him. Nothing in the world favoured their union, but he knew it was inevitable.

Mr Millar made renewed but solitary attempts during tea to include Ruth in the conversation.

"You were born in England?" he said.

"In Wales."

"I know Wales well. My father and his father did business with the Welsh. I know quite a number myself. Nice people, the Welsh," he said with a certain reservation. He was prepared to allow for the odd exception. He reeled off a list of titled landed gentry and with each name pushed Ruth further and further away from Jack's family.

If it had been his mother speaking, Jack thought, it would have been intentional. But he didn't credit his father with such subtlety. He was simply name-dropping, a favourite pastime of his.

"You're parents weren't born in Wales of course," Mr Millar went on.

"They're both Lithuanian," Ruth said.

"*Ostjuden.*" An undertone emerged from Mrs Millar's quarter between mouthfuls of home-made apple cake.

Ruth raised an eyebrow at Mr Millar. She had given up direct communication with Jack's mother.

"It doesn't matter," Jack said.

"What does it mean?" Ruth insisted.

"It means Jews from the east." Mr Millar hoped that a literal translation might satisfy her.

"I know that," Ruth said out of her meagre knowledge of German. "But does it have any other meaning? What does it imply?"

"For us," Mr Millar took the plunge, "it has a special meaning."

Ruth looked at Mrs Millar who was staring at her husband, according him the neutral role of interpreter.

"We had a lot of trouble from them in Germany," he explained. "Until they came, in their droves, we were accepted as part of German society. But they were different from us. They stuck together as if they were still living in the ghetto. The orthodox ones used to draw everyone's attention with their long beards and sideboards. And they spoke Yiddish publicly. They made themselves conspicuous, as if on purpose. They were to blame for what happened to us."

Mrs Millar nodded, approving the translation. Mr Millar had said it so calmly and with such authority that Ruth wondered whether he expected her to apologize on behalf of her section of the race who had so inconsiderately drawn attention to themselves. She looked at Jack and wondered why he made no comment. Mrs Millar was on her second piece of apple cake. Ruth looked at the diamond pendant hanging over her blouse and the ruby ring that over the years had grooved the flesh of her finger until it bordered the stone like a pie-crust. She wore her jewels no better than her own mother or her grandmother, but unlike them she fooled herself that they gave her elegance. She had not learned that elegance comes only with leisure, security and integration, such factors that had never belonged to Jews anywhere. She looked at Jack begging for some kind of observation. His silence angered her. There was a limit to loyalty and discretion. She had made enough concessions. She had worn stockings for him, and high-heeled shoes to say nothing of those dreadful white gloves. For his sake she had been silent when she should have spoken. The lying had to stop somewhere. She began to laugh, half with anger, and half with a sense of ridicule at finding herself in such company. She opened her mouth to speak, and in doing so, felt Jack's clasping hand on her wrist. He was telling her to hold her tongue. But silence was agreement and whatever she was about to sacrifice, it wasn't worth holding if she couldn't retain it with some honesty.

"But you're Jews," she said passionately. "It doesn't matter what *you* would like to think. It's other people. Hitler made no exception in your case. You were lumped with the rest of them, and you should be down on your knees every day and thanking God that you got away with your lives. There were six million who didn't," she added, almost to herself.

"We've never denied we're Jews," Mr Millar said, and everyone was surprised that he'd taken up the argument at all. "We just don't make an issue of it."

"Look," Ruth said, with terrible patience, "it's not what you do or what you think. It's what other people see in you, and it's this that is your identity. It's this you have to come to terms with."

She felt Jack's hand leave her wrist, and it seemed like a token of disengagement. She fought down a deep-seated regret that she had spoken. She loved him, and she wanted to keep him, she feared, at any price.

Mrs Millar went on eating her apple cake, but she ate mechanically. Mr Millar stared past her at the dining-room door, and there followed the kind of private silence that provokes memories seemingly disconnected with the occasion. For Jack, it was a vivid recollection of Helmuth Kahn. He was dead now, along with his parents and sister in Auschwitz, but Helmuth Kahn, although he was only thirteen, had died a man. It was a few months after his thirteenth birthday that the whole family had suddenly disappeared. Helmuth had been Jack's best friend in the Jewish school that towards the end of his stay in Germany he had been forced to attend. Helmuth had had a barmitzvah. In secrecy his family had conspired to make him a man. A few days after the ceremony, he persuaded Jack to accompany him home from school.

"I must show you my *tefillim*," he said excitedly. "I must show you how they work."

Because for Helmuth they did work, as if with magic properties. He sneaked Jack up to his bedroom and bound the leather phylacteries round his arm. As he crossed the thongs one over the other Jack noticed that a smear of bliss spread over his friend's face, a kind of look he had never seen but had often felt on his own face during his dreams.

"When I put them on," Helmuth whispered, as if he didn't want the straps to know, "I get excited." He wondered whether he was making himself clear. "Inside me," he stammered. He didn't want to be too clear about it all.

Jack nodded his head. He felt a faint surge of envy. He wanted a go too, but he knew he was not entitled to share Helmuth's discovery.

"I put them on four or five times a day," Helmuth was saying. "I'm not supposed to," he giggled, "but they sort of do things inside of me."

He raised his eyebrows at Jack. He needed him to understand what he was trying to say. Slowly he removed the leather.

"It works every time I put it on. It's 'cos I'm a man, see."

There was a tone of slight spite in his voice. Jack was tempted to snatch the phylacteries from him and to prove that they would work for him too, but he knew he was taking too big a risk. He wanted to get out of the room. He wanted to get home into his own little bedroom and sit on his bed and hate his mother. She had let his thirteenth birthday go by without any extra ceremony or initiation. She had cheated him out of manhood, while all his friends at school had suddenly become men. Their dreams as boys had become dreams of the grown-up, and though they were still the same dreams, manhood had sanctioned them. Certain thoughts they now had a right to, whereas in boyhood these same thoughts were obscene.

Jack looked at Ruth and for a moment he had to recollect

who she was. Then he realized that it was she, and his need for her, that had occasioned his recollection of Helmuth Kahn. He was suddenly convinced that somehow, if he had been given a barmitzvah, he could have loved Ruth freely and without the need of his mother's hostility. He laid his hands on the table, and felt a vein of anger protrude on his forehead.

"Why," he practically shouted at his mother, "why didn't I have a barmitzvah?"

He saw his mother smile softly behind her apple cake, and he heard his father cough. He didn't want an answer. He had only needed to voice his private fears. He wanted Ruth to hear them too, although he knew that she understood them already. He wanted to let his parents know that they were to blame. It was not Ruth's fault that she was too much of a woman for him. It was theirs that they had not equipped him to confront her. He gripped Ruth's wrist again. He had made an uneasy pact with her.

The meal was passively consumed. Ruth nudged her feet into the shoes that she'd kicked off under the table.

"We must go," she heard Jack say, and she got up and stood behind him. She watched him as he kissed his mother and tremblingly stroked her arm.

"Thank her," he hissed savagely to Ruth as he passed across her.

The formalities of leave-taking were polite and precise, and soon Jack and Ruth found themselves outside the front door. He took her arm, and pointed to the jamb of the white door-frame. On it was a small oblong patch. It was whiter than the surrounding wood and the nail holes that framed it showed that something had once been there and had been removed.

"Look," he said bitterly. "This house belonged to Jews

before my father bought it. The first thing he did when he moved in was to take it off."

The scar on the lintel was as compelling as the symbol that had once covered it, like a lie that is often as revealing as the truth it conceals. "Do not pass us over," the white wound shrieked. "Include us in, for God's sake."

# 2

"Mom," Ruth yelled.

Her voice carried down the terrace of houses. She knew their front door would be open and her mother in the kitchen and that door open too. She gave her a few seconds to come to the front gate, and there suddenly she was, aproned and waving, a ladle in her hand, joined by a dribble of neighbours to whom the cry of 'Mom' was equally un-answerable.

She tugged at Jack's sleeve. Compared with the demands he had made on her when taking her to his parents, she had asked little of him. He was to talk about his writing. Her father would like that. And he was to underplay his parents' titled connections which would not have gone down well at all. She had coached him in the most elementary of Hebrew terms, mainly the names of the festivals, and had listed the names of a few Jewish writers so that he would not be com-pletely at sea when her father extolled their virtues. During the lessons his ignorance of Jewish matters frightened her and once again she had tried to understand why she loved him. Their incompatability was beyond challenge or resolu-tion, but their mutual and desperate recognition of it made it almost compatible. In desperation he had taken her to his parents, and with the same desperation she was taking him to hers.

"Don't forget to tell them about my room," she whispered urgently.

He was to reassure her parents that she was leading a decent clean life in her room the other side of London, and that it was quite natural for a girl to set up on her own as soon as she started working. He must say he was keeping an eye on her anyway, but not too proximate an eye, he must make that clear.

They reached the house. The neighbours took Jack in with as long a glance as curiosity short of rudeness permitted, and returned to their own kitchens.

"You ate?" Mrs Lazarus asked. First things first.

"We had a snack," Ruth said. But she was already hungry. She always had room for a meal at her mother's table as if her stomach reserved a special pocket for her hospitality.

"A snack," Mrs Lazarus snorted. "Who eats snacks? You eat or you don't eat. Simple. Come, there's plenty. Fish, salad, soup. Plenty I have. Always in the house is plenty."

They followed her into the kitchen. The rest of the family were already seated, and Jack had the feeling that they had been seated since the last meal. The two boys, David and Paul, were unmaking a jigsaw, spreading the pieces separately over the white cloth so as to start it all over again. Mr Lazarus put down his Yiddish newspaper. He beamed a huge smile. "Ruthele," he said. He half rose, and leaned over the table to kiss her, brushing the jigsaw pieces into disorder.

"Look what you've done, Pop. Messed it up again," David shouted. Neither of the boys was interested in the newcomer.

"Jigsaws, jigsaws," Mr Lazarus smiled, "all they think of, jigsaws. Ten guineas a term I pay for piano lessons. Do they touch it? Never. Mention a Hebrew lesson and they run. Goyim, my sons," he smiled, ruffling David's hair. He put his hand on Jack's shoulder, fingering the cloth on the sleeve. As a tailor Mr Lazarus would never pass up an opportunity of examining another contractor's work. He had inwardly to admit that Jack's shoulder was skilfully built, but the cloth, well, he could get better.

"This is Jack," Ruth pushed him towards her father.

"Who else?" Mr Lazarus said. "Every day on the telephone she talks Jack, Jack. Sit down if you can find room."

Mr Lazarus stretched out his arm and made a clean sweep of the jigsaw pieces. David and Paul, unsurprised by his gesture, followed the falling wooden shapes to the floor, where they remained squatting on their heels and re-assembling, until Mrs Lazarus put the steaming bowls of soup on the table. Jack waited until she served herself, but she made no move and Jack noticed that there was not even a place laid for her.

"Mom never sits down," Ruth explained. "She hovers."

Mrs Lazarus stood behind each of them in turn, mimicking the action of their soup-tasting.

"Is good?" she kept saying, after each mouthful.

"You want more?" she said, although they had barely started. "There's plenty." She circled the table throughout the course, ladle in hand, vicariously relishing her cooking. "Smells good," she said inviting more compliments. "Smells very good."

"Mom," Ruth said patiently, "why don't you sit down and have some?"

Mrs Lazarus laughed. "All day I'm eating," she said. "I'm not fat enough for you?" She pummelled the extra layers of fat on her arms, testimony to years of daily soup tasting. "You eat and enjoy," she said. She pounced on Mr

Lazarus as he scooped up his last spoonful. "More?" she threatened him. He handed her his plate meekly and Mrs Lazarus triumphantly ladled an extra helping.

"Swop you a knedle for a go on your bike after supper?" Paul whispered to David.

A knedle was a big sacrifice, but a go on David's bike was worth every lost mouthful. David considered the bargain.

"For five minutes," he said. He was not open to an offer.

"Ten?" Paul pleaded. It was a big knedle.

"Take it or leave it."

Under cover of his other hand, Paul attempted to pass the knedle over. Mrs Lazarus missed nothing.

"So," she said, laying down her ladle. "Not good enough for you, your mother's cooking?"

Paul preferred she knew the truth, rather than have her suspect he'd gone off her knedle.

"I'm swopping it for a go on his bike after supper."

"After supper," Mr Lazarus settled the matter, "is Hebrew lesson. After barmitzvah, bikes perhaps."

Paul retrieved his knedle. His father's word was law.

"Another six months," Mr Lazarus explained to Jack, "and three men we'll have in the house. Two of them with jigsaws still."

The conversation now threatened to move into unfamiliar ground and Jack shifted uneasily.

"Bet you don't remember your *pasha*, Jack?"

Mr Lazarus laughed. Jack had no idea what it was, but he assumed that it was in some way connected with a barmitzvah.

"I didn't have one," he said.

It was a bad beginning. No amount of knowledge of Jewish writers or history could compensate for lack of initiation.

"You were ill?" Mrs Lazarus was anxious to give him some loop-hole.

"No," he said. "At the time of my thirteenth birthday, things were very bad in Germany and we couldn't do anything about it."

It sounded very feeble. God would have forgiven a postponement, Mr Lazarus thought. In those days, countless fourteen and fifteen year-olds turned up in some synagogue or another to keep their tardy appointment.

"So you never had one," Mr Lazarus was forced to confirm. "But you would have," he said hopefully, "if you'd been able."

"Yes," Jack agreed eagerly. "I feel I missed something. I suppose my mother could have done something about it in England."

He was glad to shift the responsibility. He didn't consider the omission as anything to do with his father. His father hadn't had one either. Perhaps that was his problem too.

Mrs Lazarus had refilled his soup plate while he was speaking. Paul and David had already started on the fish. There was no ceremony at the Lazarus' table. All courses were serveable at the same time. This lack of ceremony and the resultant disorganization pleased Jack and he compared it sullenly with the cold order of his mother's house. Between each dish at his mother's table lay a decent interval, a digestive breathing space. Each set place owned its own starched white napkin, whereas at the Lazarus' table one time-honoured rag at the centre of the table was common property, and cutlery used for one course was wiped on it and used for the next. Fish was eaten with a soup spoon if no forks were handy, and hunks of bread were torn from the plaited loaf on the bread board. Wine, at home, was drunk in hock or claret glasses; at the Lazarus', orange squash came in tea-cups. Sauces at his mother's house had bouquet and steamed from sauce-boats; here they stood processed and labelled in crusted-topped bottles.

Mrs Lazarus hovered behind Paul and David for their verdict on the fish.

"Not as good as Grandma's," David said.

It was the only criticism permissible in the house. In fact, Mrs Lazarus took it as a compliment.

"When I'm a grandma, please God," she lapped Ruth and Jack into an eyeful, "I also shall make better fish. Gefullte fish is practice. What does your mother use, Jack, for gefullte fish?"

"We've never had it," he said, without realizing the enormity of his confession. Mrs Lazarus put down her ladle.

"Perhaps your grandmother?" she said hopefully.

Jack shook his head. The lack of a barmitzvah was one thing, and at a stretch, excusable. But an ignorance of gefullte fish suggested omissions in Jack's background which were unpardonable. Such ignorance ruled out the whole ritual on Friday night, which, without gefullte fish, was barely celebrateable. Gefullte fish was not just a common sea food. In Jewish terms it was an essential ingredient of a way of life. Both Jack's mother and his grandmother had managed to survive without it. There was no doubt that Ruth's new find came from a shamelessly filleted lineage.

Mr Lazarus accepted Jack's new found inadequacy in silence. He put aside his soup plate and helped himself to the subject of their conversation. The silence was almost unbearable. Only the two boys, intent on their food, seemed indifferent. Jack put his arm round Ruth's shoulder.

"I hope Ruth can make it, Mrs Lazarus."

He wanted to show at least his willingness to co-operate.

Mrs Lazarus smiled. His gesture towards Ruth moved her, and she looked at her husband shyly.

"Where should she learn? In her bed-sitting room? A good home she leaves. God knows what she cooks for herself. I tell you," she leaned across the table, "for the university she went to, I'm not sorry, for the letters after her name, I'm proud, believe me. That she's a teacher, also I'm not sorry, but that she should leave a good home, for that, I'm sorry."

The boys joined in the chorus of her last apology. It was a speech they had heard many times before. Ruth nudged Jack under the table. It was his cue and he took it up gratefully. The conversation was shifting to more familiar ground.

"She cooks very well for herself," Jack said. "And anyway, it's good for a girl to live on her own when she's working. It teaches her independence."

He himself was not over-convinced by this theory, but he had to get away from the subject of food. He was terrified that the old fish would threaten the conversation again with yet other ritual dishes of which he was ignorant.

"It's not as if she never comes home," he went on. "She's always excited when she comes over to see you."

"Once a week, if we're lucky, she comes home for a decent meal," Mrs Lazarus complained. Here it was again. Jack turned it away neatly.

"It's not only a question of food, Mrs Lazarus."

He was determined to put the damn fish out of the conversation once and for all.

"She comes here for the family life," he said.

"Once a week?" Mr Lazarus asked.

"It's nothing to do with how often. It's the feeling of

family connection. If she only came once a month, it would still be as strong."

He realized for the first time the salient difference between them. Ruth was included. In his own family he was, like his parents, an outsider, a spectator of a theoretical unit that just wasn't there.

Mrs Lazarus pushed the fish dish towards him. It pointed at him like a dagger, and he waited for further reference to his ignorance, but Mr Lazarus interrupted the silence with, "Ruth tells me you write," he said. Jack could have hugged him.

"Yes," Jack said. "It's what I want to do finally. I write poetry but I've started a novel."

As he said it, he realized he had opened the door to yet another trap and quickly he recapped to himself the list of Yiddish writers Ruth had armed him with.

"What writers do you admire?" he asked, plunging right into the fray.

"I'm old-fashioned," Mr Lazarus said. "I read the old ones. Peretz, Nordau, Sholom Aleichem."

The list was familiar. He had even learned them in the same order.

"D'you read any English writers?"

"Again the old ones. I read poetry sometimes in English. Tennyson, Wordsworth. I'd like to read yours," he said; "but I don't promise I shall understand it," he added humbly.

"Nu?"

Mrs Lazarus stood behind them like a giant hovercraft, awaiting their verdict.

"It's as good as usual," Ruth said, trying to take the responsibility for both of them. She wanted Jack to go on talking to her father.

"I'd love to show you some of my poems," Jack said.

"Have you read Bialik?" Mr Lazarus asked.

Ruth had slipped up. It was a name completely unfamiliar to him.

"No," he stammered.

"But you've heard of him?" Mr Lazarus's voice was slightly raised.

Jack felt he should plead guilty straight away. There was no point in flannelling with Mr Lazarus.

"No, I haven't," he said airily, as if it were not such a terrible sin.

Mr Lazarus was silent again. He recapped the monotonous list of Jack's inadequacies, and realized sadly that his daughter was on the point of marrying out.

Mrs Lazarus ladled stewed fruit into bowls and put them in front of Paul and David.

"Hurry up," she said, "and finish. Grandma and Auntie Sal will be here soon. They can sit in your places."

"They're coming?" Mr Lazarus asked. "I hope he's not coming too."

"He" was Auntie Sal's husband, whom nobody, least of all Auntie Sal, got on with. But when he was attacked in the family circle, and usually with justification, Auntie Sal was overcome by a quaint sense of loyalty, and she would defend him. It was her vociferous yet feeble defence of her mate that Mr Lazarus found most irritating of all.

"Also a writer," Mrs Lazarus explained to Jack, as if he'd know by that fact exactly what to expect of Auntie Sal's husband.

"Except," Mr Lazarus went on, "he doesn't write. Ever. Not a line. He sits. He thinks. Well, he sits anyway. All days he sits, and God forbid anyone should ask him to do something. A lazy good-for-nothing that Hymy. I hope for everybody's sake, he doesn't come."

Hymy was the first to enter the kitchen through the ever-open front door. He was followed by Grandma on the arm of Auntie Sal.

"Sit, sit." Mrs Lazarus directed them to the boy's places with her ladle. Hymy didn't need a second invitation. He lifted David bodily off his chair, together with his unfinished fruit, and sat in his place.

"What did I tell you?" Mr Lazarus turned to Jack. Then to Hymy.

"You can't wait? Believe me, the fish won't run away."

And Jack was inclined to agree with him. There was plenty more where that came from. The fish was there for ever.

"I'll get another chair," he said, rising.

"In the dining-room," Mrs Lazarus said, with absolute conviction that he knew where it was. She already thought of him as a longstanding member of the family.

He found himself in a large room. A round table stood in the centre and on it a silver three-fingered candlestick. In its shadow, a Hebrew bible lay open, and a silver pointer lay in the folds of the book. The double spread of the open page was worn thin with thumb marks and pin points, and the leaves had stretched beyond the normal width of the book. Jack looked at the well-studied page. It was obviously the portion of the law that David would read at his barmitzvah. He leafed through the book and shortly came across a similar double-spread, stretched over the edge, pock-marked and thumb-worn. Paul's piece of a year ago. The pattern of the letters on the page was meaningless to him and he bitterly resented what he had been denied. He felt an ache of unbelonging. He grabbed a chair and dragged it from the table. As he passed the sideboard he saw an old rolled up photograph. As he unrolled it, it smeared into four or five hundred uniformed girls, the centre decently spread with well-combed mousy staff. In the left corner was an undeniable blotch of black hair interrupted by the creases of laughter. She had changed very little, and although her hands were behind her back, he knew that the finger nails were dirty. He couldn't imagine a time when he had not known or loved her, or indeed, her family, with whose warmth he felt a stifled and forbidden contact. His mother would have felt threatened by the Lazarus's unassailable sense of identity, and she would have pitied them for their stubborn and separate ways. He would have to marry Ruth if only to spite his mother.

He carried the chair into the kitchen. Grandma had meanwhile taken his place, and he saw that he was to be separated from Ruth. He sat at the table and his plate was passed over to him. He felt he was being stared at. In the silence, Grandma, Auntie Sal and Uncle Hymy were viewing the body. Grandma finally broke the silence with a question directed at Jack in Yiddish. Jack looked around him helplessly. Another mark against him.

"She wants to know your verdict on Mom's fish," Ruth told him.

"Tell her it's wonderful," Jack said, "but I hear that hers is better."

He suddenly felt secure. With Ruth as his interpreter, he was removed from the damn fish once and for all. He would leave it to Ruth to edit his answers and so absolve him from further embarrassment. She would look after his reactions and temper them accordingly. He hoped Grandma would go on talking forever. But alas, she had started into her fish while her daughter hovered shyly behind her.

Hymy stretched his arm the length of the table to pick up his portion.

"You can't ask?" Mr Lazarus said. Stretching across others at the Lazarus's table was normal procedure, but for Hymy, Mr Lazarus made different rules.

"Manners you're wanting?" Hymy said. "Please," he mocked, "would you be so kind as to pass me the fish dish?"

"*Chaser*," Mr Lazarus muttered.

Hymy stretched across to Mr Lazarus until their faces were almost touching.

"What was that?" he said.

"Pig," Mr Lazarus said.

He looked at Auntie Sal and saw that she was arming.

"And I don't want any excuses from you," Mr Lazarus went on. "In my house he behaves."

"All of a sudden," Hymy said, "the Lazarus family are civilized. Ah," he looked at Jack, "I see the reason."

Mr Lazarus had had enough of Hymy. He was angry too with his wife for having asked him. A stream of abuse flooded his mind, but because of Jack's presence and for Ruth's sake, he decided on a quick précis. His mouth full of fish, he spluttered across the room, "Shut up."

Mrs Lazarus, ladle in hand, calmly removed the evidence of fish spray from the table, the mantelpiece and the opposite wall. Then she ladled her husband his dish of stewed fruit.

Somebody had to say something. As an outsider, Jack was allowed a certain neutrality. He turned to Hymy.

"Are you a writer?" he said.

"Yes, I'm a writer," Hymy said with the sort of conviction that no real writer could ever achieve.

"D'you write novels?"

"Yes. I've written four," Hymy said largely, "but I've put them aside. I'm not very happy with them." He shrugged his shoulders by way of apology to a reading public that was denied his literary genius.

"My standards are pretty high," he added, and it sounded like a warning.

"What writers d'you admire?" Jack tried again.

He didn't want to lose Hymy so soon. The fish course was still going strong on the table, and it would have to disappear before he could relax completely.

"None, I'm afraid," Hymy said sadly. He waved his hand with the lame authority of a man who had read nothing. He too was anxious to change the subject.

"Not even the Russians?" Jack pressed on.

"Oh, they're all right," Hymy said generously, not knowing quite who the Russians were.

Grandma had finished her fish and Auntie Sal helped herself to the remaining piece on the dish. Things were easing up. Once more, Grandma addressed herself to Jack.

"She wants to know," Ruth said, "if you're in business."

Grandma knew that fundamental enquiries had not been made. Her daughter had skimmed around the surfaces and her son-in-law had probably done the same. It was up to her to get down to the hard facts. Ruth was her first grandchild. She was going to have a say in marrying her off.

"He's a teacher, Grandma," Ruth said.

Grandma was visibly unimpressed. "And his father?"

"He's in textiles."

Grandma smiled slyly. That was better. Jack leaned back, gratefully opting out of the conversation. Ruth was adequately equipped to deal with it.

"His father's business isn't good enough for him?"

Grandma said. She too had excluded Jack from the conversation.

"He doesn't like business," Ruth said. Then with a deep breath, "He's going to be a writer."

Grandma shuddered so that Hymy trembled. "One too many already I've got in the family. And you will work all your life like your Auntie Sal. A no-good he is." She withered Hymy across the table. "Words, words," she said with contempt, "the best seller, my fat arse."

This last in English and Jack shuddered at the entirely unexpected vulgarity. He hoped it wasn't directed at him, but he saw Grandma smiling at him, and he pitied poor Hymy who was the only alternative for her scorn.

"Look, Momma," Auntie Sal spoke for the first time, and it sounded like "Look Momma for the thousandth time, did you marry him or did I? Do I work for him, or do you?"

"You married him," Grandma stayed in English — such a partnership was even sourer in Yiddish — "Yes, you work for him, like a dog you work for him, but who suffers, I'm asking? I suffer. For him, no. But for you, for my own daughter, she should throw herself away on such rubbish, for that I suffer."

She talked as if Hymy wasn't there and Hymy was happy to pretend he wasn't. He stretched over the table for another piece of fish, found the dish empty and glared at Auntie Sal's half eaten portion with accusation. She forked it off her plate and handed it to him. She would give up everything for him, her food, her bed and her time, but she would hang on to her suffering for ever.

"Go on," Grandma said to her, "lie on the floor. Let him step on you." And Hymy, with an ominous sense of deprivation swallowed his fish whole.

"Feh," Grandma spat at him.

"Momma!" Auntie Sal opened her mouth in defence.

"With writing you don't make a living," Grandma announced her findings to the table. The evidence was there for everyone to see. A prime example on their own doorstep.

"Your Jack must go into business with his father," she decided. "A wife, a family, please God, need money. Only in your own business is money." She had already retired Mr Millar senior. Mrs Lazarus hovered silently with her ladle, and Mr Lazarus concentrated on his stewed prunes.

"D'you hear?" Grandma almost shouted, desperately trying to include them in her own sense of urgency, "he must go into business."

Jack had a sense of in absentia, and for a moment he felt a great affinity with Hymy.

Ruth rose uncomfortably from the table. She resented the shame she felt for her family and she had to get out of the room quickly.

"Jack and I'll do the washing-up," she said.

"Such a good idea," said Mrs Lazarus, who also wanted the conversation to end. But it made no difference to Grandma that the subjects of her concern were not present. She was going to make her point just the same. All of them were a little afraid of Grandma. Even Mr Lazarus bowed to her authority, but such matters as his son-in-law's income or prospects seemed to him too private to investigate. He knew that it had to be done, and he did not resent Grandma taking over the job. He just wished she would handle it more subtly. She was almost crude.

"You want that Ruth should have a family?" Grandma rambled on as Ruth and Jack cleared the table. "On words she should feed them? On typewriters?"

Ruth shut the scullery door. She tried to make as much

noise as possible with the dishes, but still her grandmother's voice strained through the door, joined by an occasional scream from Auntie Sal, a groan from the absent Hymy, and an intermittent "Shah, shah" from her father. She hated them all. She hated their public way of living, and she wished to God she had never brought Jack to the house. For a moment she longed for the cold sense of detachment that Jack had with his own parents. She turned both taps full on trying to drown the noise of the ugly squabbling behind the door. But Jack wanted to listen. Not necessarily to what was said; he wanted to be part of their noise of contact. He compared it with the cold silence of his mother's house, and he felt cheated. He envied the Lazaruses' demonstrative affection, their rich and angry quarrels, and the tensed uneasy truce. For him, the Lazaruses were alive and furious with a love that he in his mother's frigid drawing room had never experienced. He turned to Ruth and held her hiding from the noise, in his arms. They would each marry what they considered their own deepest inadequacy, hers for freedom, his for inclusion.

When they left, Mr Lazarus gave his verdict.

"A nice boy, but she's almost marrying out, Chayala," he said.

Mrs Lazarus, still with her ladle, nodded sadly. Across London and into the suburbs, Mr and Mrs Millar had given the same verdict, but only Ruth and Jack knew how out they were marrying.

## 3

After a few weeks, the Lazaruses came to terms with the fact that their daughter was serious, and with little appetite they made preparations for the wedding. One of the first moves was to announce it in the Jewish paper. An official announcement would make it a reality, and Mr Lazarus was entrusted with the insertion.

On the Friday when the paper came out, Mrs Lazarus opened it warily, dreading to find that the rumours were true. Her husband had put it in the Social and Personal column of the paper, the four guinea column, as it was known, where births, marriages and deaths were to be taken more seriously. Mrs Lazarus turned to the appropriate page. Every week, when the paper came out, she turned to this page, reassuring herself that even though Jews had died, God rest their souls, Jews had been born, and Jews had married Jews to beget Jews. Her reading of the page gave her weekly confidence in her survival. She tackled the births first. An Anthea had been born, an Alistair, a Penelope, a Victoria, an Oliver and an Edwina; all good solid, English names and Mrs Lazarus didn't like them, even though they appeared in the four guinea column. She remembered during the war and just before it, how the column was proudly filled with Aarons and Esthers and Miriams and Sauls. A reasonably accurate account of the history of the Jewish people could be gauged by the names of the newly-born in the four guinea column of the paper. In times of crisis, when pogroms threatened and persecution was rife, the Jews reaffirmed their faith with the births of Davids and Sarahs. The moment the pressure was off, Alistairs were born, along with Edwinas.

Mrs Lazarus turned gingerly to the engagement column. It was the birth column of twenty or so years ago, and naturally dotted with crisis names. Sadie was going to marry Samuel, and Brina was promised to Aaron. Rachel would love and honour Yitzchak, and Ruth Lazarus was lined up for Jack Millar. Mrs Lazarus stared at the notice for a long time.

Mr and Mrs Millar ignored all Jack's pleas to come to the wedding, with the firm intention of accepting the invitation at the last moment. They had no doubt that their son was making a mistake, not for his sake – that was unimportant – but he had let his family down, who had for generations married into their own kind. They would go to the wedding if only as a reminder to their son of the standards of life he was rejecting. And they went, like royalty on a visit to the slums.

If the Lazaruses had had misgivings about their daughter's marriage before the wedding, they were only increased by their introduction to Jack's parents. The Millars and the Lazaruses met for the first time at the ceremony, and both parties quietly determined that they would never meet each other again. Each gave their verdict on the other, and each verdict was precisely the same. "They're not our kind of people", was what the Millars said of the Lazaruses, and more vociferously, Ruth's parents of Jack's.

After the wedding, when they were alone, Jack looked at Ruth and took stock of her. He gathered her loose hair into a bun, pulling it roughly into a semblance of neatness. He opened her clenched fist and noted the dirty nails with little surprise. But her newly ringed finger stupefied him, as he realized with horror what he had done. He gripped her in his arms and kissed her violently, trying to stifle the unbearable thought that though he loved her, she was not his kind of person.

They went to Paris after the wedding, and the following day, once they were settled in the hotel and alone, Jack felt an unaccountable desire to go home. He wanted to be with Ruth, but here in a strange bedroom, and away from the known places of his bachelorhood, he felt in a vacuum, and Ruth had become too isolated a figure to be taken seriously as his wife. When they went down to dinner, she noticed his increasing agitation.

"Why are you so restless?" she said.

He was angry that she had noticed it. "I'm not," he laughed it off. "I'm just hungry, I suppose."

They said very little to each other during the meal, and when it was over, Ruth leaned across the table and put her hand on his.

"D'you want to go home?" she said.

Jack had had hints of her mind-reading talents during their courting-days, but he had never considered them as a threat.

"It's a wrench cutting oneself off from one day to the next," Ruth was saying.

It wasn't her intuition that disturbed him, so much as her understanding. He didn't particularly want to be understood, at least not in the areas of his own privacy. He forced another laugh.

"I think I can take care of myself," he said. "And you," he added, "if you want me to."

She smiled. "Lots of people curtail their honeymoons," she said.

"Who said I wanted to go home?" he practically shouted at her.

Nevertheless, the following day, with an unspoken love and relief between them, they came back to London.

# 4

Ruth had given up her job. She wanted to create conditions in which their partnership could achieve permanence, for their incompatability sometimes frightened her. Jack decided to go into his father's business. The fait accompli of their union remained a mystery to him. He did not know how it had happened any more than he knew that it was inevitable. The marriage was a trap into which both of them had volunteered, and they set about to elaborate their prison and make it even more secure. So Ruth became a housewife, and Jack an earning business man, a joint root of a potential family. With money from Ruth's parents, they put a down payment on a rambling house, thus furnishing their prison with parental obligation. They acquired pictures and furniture, and endless 'things' for the mantelpiece, which objects, in the long run, make divorce so inconvenient. Unwittingly they secured themselves in their deep and precarious love for each other. Hell was a way of living as long as there was no hole in it.

Out of their love they teased each other about their incompatabilities. Each visit to Jack's or Ruth's parents underlined their differences. Jack's mother would never in a lifetime take to her son's choice, but she entertained them coldly and formally. Jack gloried in her hostility, and backed by it, was able to love Ruth more deeply. And it was partly for this need of continued contact with his mother that he had entered his father's business.

In Germany, the family business had dealt in leather, but on his arrival in England Mr Millar had enlarged his scope. He dealt first in other materials and finally branched out into a small wholesale dress business. It was to this section of the business that he sent Jack for training and eventual take-over. Jack hated it. Not so much the work, though it left him little enough time for his writing, but because of his daily contact with his father. All his married life, Mr Millar senior had been ruled by his wife, and now he had an opportunity of playing the same role himself regarding his son. He never ceased to remind Jack of his obligations, how, by dint of his own hard work over the years, he, his son, was able to enter a flourishing business. How Jack would benefit financially, and how Jack's wife who had never known the good things of life, could benefit too. It was a daily sermon that Jack suffered from his father and all through the day he anticipated with joy his return to Ruth.

Each evening she was waiting, the table laid with cutlery, glass and serviettes. She made every effort to compromise on certain of their differences, but inwardly Jack found her efforts irritating. Side-plates and serviettes were not an intrinsic part of Ruth's psyche, yet their absence irritated him even more. He did not want her to lose her identity on his behalf, though he made constant demands on her and when she gave in and compromised, he disliked her a little.

One such occasion was his mother's birthday, a few months after their marriage. Jack and Ruth were sent an invitation card to take tea at the Millar house. An unstamped reply card was appended. Jack phoned his mother to say that they would both be there.

He waited for her in the living room. "Hurry up," he called, "we'll be late."

She appeared at the doorway. "I'm ready," she said.

She held out the white gloves that were a prerequisite for a visit to his mother's house, and smiled at him.

"You look beautiful," he said coming towards her. He kissed her and she walked on ahead to the front door. Then he noticed for the first time her bare legs.

"Go and put stockings on," he exploded, deeply insulted on his mother's behalf.

Ruth turned round. She held out the gloves again as a symbol of how far she was prepared to go.

"It's high summer," she said coldly. "I'm not wearing stockings in this weather."

"Go and put them on," he shouted. He wasn't prepared to argue about the relevance of the season.

"No."

He grabbed her arm, twisting it. It was the first time he had been violent with her, and he shivered at the thrill it gave him.

"Your hair is loose," he hissed at her, "and that's enough. Go and put stockings on."

"No," she whispered through the pain.

He threw her on to the hall floor, and kicked her thigh as she lay there stupefied.

"It's late," he shouted, horrified by what he'd done, but he went on relentlessly. "Put them on. We're already late."

He kicked her again and she made no move to get up. He hoped fervently that she would not give in to him, that an argument would develop, that she would insult him and his family so that his behaviour could be retrospectively excused. But she got up meekly and went upstairs into the bedroom. When she came down he did not dare to look at her legs.

"Are my seams straight?" she said without questioning. He couldn't bring himself to apologize to her. The following day, he bought her an expensive dress, his first contribution to what was to become a wardrobe of his conscience.

He noticed that his bouts of violence were almost always occasioned by some reference to his mother, and that after they were over, he was able, without fear or challenge to face Ruth and to love her. He wondered what would happen to their marriage if his mother died. He loved Ruth enough. It wasn't that. When he looked at her, sitting opposite him at their dining-table, he felt an enormous joy that she was there. But he was convinced that after the meal she would get up and go home. Even after a few months of marriage, he retained this conviction, and each time it was shattered, as, after the meal was finished, Ruth would gather up the dishes and begin to wash up. She lives here, he would suddenly realize, she washes my clothes, she shares my bed, she knows my toothbrush as well as she knows her own; she has seen me sweat; she has heard me snore; she has timed me in the bathroom; she has stalked my privacy and she doesn't even think it is private.

He followed her into the kitchen and watched her as she washed the dishes. The plates from the preceding meal were still in the sink, and a number of dirty rags cluttered the draining board.

"Why aren't you a bit more organized?" he said patiently.

He thought of his mother, for whom the occasional washing up was a ceremony, attended by rubber gloves, a sink of bubbling foam, and an assortment of coloured sponges. Ruth's washing up habits were inherited from her mother. In the Lazarus's home, Jack had noticed, washing up was never a ritual performance. It was done in instalments, between other things and never with bubbles or gloves or white tiles. Instead, a stone floor, a rotting wood draining board, open shelves, a grey-stone sink and a brown-panelled door, firmly shut against all labour-saving devices except labour.

Jack picked up one of the rags from the board, and holding it high between his fingers, he dropped it into the dustbin.

"Why did you do that?" Ruth said.

"We can afford a new dish-cloth."

It was the waste that offended her and the terrible finality of throwing something away. She thought nostalgically of her mother, how she would wash down the draining board with an old rag, that had, in its hey-day, been an embroidered oven-cloth. With the present holder of that title, she would draw out the roast chicken from the oven, her red face averted, puffing and sighing. And there would come a moment when she would examine the oven-cloth and the draining board rag, separately and comparatively, and decide that the time had come for demotion. The draining-board rag was suddenly and without ceremony assigned to floor-washing and the oven-cloth to the draining board. The floor was rock-bottom. After that, even in Mrs Lazarus's domestic economy, there was no place for it except the dustbin. But her mother would never herself put it there. That it was useless she would not deny, but she wanted no part in its burial. It was Ruth or Mr Lazarus who, understanding her aversion to finality would, without comment, arrange for its disposal.

One of Ruth's most salient memories of her childhood, was this hierarchy of dusters in the Lazarus household. Each time she saw one assigned to the dustbin, she wondered where and how it had started. And she had discovered that its origins varied. It might have started off very respectably as one of her father's vests. Or perhaps her mother's stocking. And via the better furniture, the oven, the draining-board and the floor, she had witnessed its slow and sad decline to the dustbin. What was certain was that whatever its genesis it had never originated as a full-blown, professional, all-exclusive duster. She remembered the Millar's kitchen and the pile of clean coloured squares on the top shelf, soft, absorbent. On the draining-board were an assortment of coloured sponges and magnetically stuck to the oven were patchwork gloves. She wondered sadly what Mrs Millar did with all her husband's old vests and her own torn stockings, and concluded that once they had lost their original function they were thrown away. Her mother had more respect for inanimate things.

She shuddered at the differences between them. In order to consider Jack as a partner, she had to strip him of his history. She dismissed the vast spaces between them and looked at him standing alongside her. She saw him simply as the man she loved, a happening, immaculate and unsired.

He turned back to the living room. He wanted desperately to be alone. Ruth was a challenge that frightened him. He was ashamed of how badly he sometimes treated her. But always she understood and the burden of her decency was sometimes unbearable. When he was away from her, he imagined her with frenzied anticipation, but the flesh and blood of her, her being and her looking so much of a woman, fed his fears of his own inadequacy. "God," he thought, "if only she would cut her hair."

He looked around the room and his eye fell on the skirting board beside him. A thin layer of dust coated the rim, and no doubt continued behind the radiogram which shielded it. In the joint of the wall, a few feet from the ground, was a cobweb. It fitted snugly into the niche, a work of many hours duration, bolstered by layers of dust on each side, with the spider working his way around, smugly and with confidence, for all the world as if the site were freehold. Jack watched it intently. He saw it in one position and then another, and although he never took his eyes off it, he never saw it move. Further up the joint of the wall was another cobweb, fully completed, with vacant possession. The spider was obviously a contractor and Jack wondered what he could hope to profit from his long hours of work on such a fruitless site. Was it that he couldn't help himself? Jack wanted to touch it, to let his fingers throb against the drive in its spindly legs, to trace the dewy filigree in its slow and steady orbit, to become himself part of the endeavour, even a necessary part. After all, it was his house, wasn't it, it was by his good leave that the spider was there at all. He stretched his fingers towards the web, trembling. But no matter how far he pushed his hand the web receded and the wall with it, remote, untouchable. He stared at his trembling fingers and then at the spider he knew he loved so tenderly, and between the one and the other there budged a paralysis that was almost tangible.

"Ruth," he shouted, "why can't you keep this place clean?"

She carried the tray of coffee to the table.

"What is it?" she said patiently.

"The place is filthy."

"Where?" said Ruth, looking around. A superficial examination of the room proved it to be spotless.

"The silver's clean, the carpet's hoovered, everything's polished, the curtains are washed." Whatever Jack had to complain about she was going to make it sound pretty trivial.

"What about the cobwebs on the wall?"

"I know about them," she said, "They've been here for weeks. There's another one in that corner over there that you haven't noticed. I like them. They make the place look like home. I like them and they're staying."

Jack went out of the room and returned very quickly armed with a sweeping brush. He went from one niche of the wall to the other, running the brush up the join with a ruthless destructive joy. A few thin, disjointed threads of dust hung from the wall, like the skeleton of a house after a bomb had fallen. And these too he swept away, gathering the rubble on the end of his brush like a conquerer. Although the work did not greatly tax his strength he was sweating profusely. The thin pathetic cobwebs on the wall were to him all that he had never achieved, and was fast losing hope of achieving. All that he wanted and would never cease to want; a means of expression as irresistible and compulsive as that of a spider. And why couldn't he? He considered the question for a moment, holding the brush upright in his hand. Why couldn't he what? He didn't know. He was conscious only of a great 'why' in his mind. Of something that had at the least to be questioned, of something unfinished, or erringly begun. His work? He made use of all the free time he had. That did not worry him. Ruth? He loved her. In the end and in the beginning of things he loved her. Why was he too guilty to be happy. Why was he silent, yet his mouth so chock-a-block full with vocabulary? Why were the palms of his hands itching to enclose, to love, to protect. He saw Ruth sitting there, upright, and he knew that his arm-rests round her shoulders were cold and waiting. That perhaps inside her, he hoped, writhing through her body, was another great 'why'. He moved, or thought he moved, towards her, but again between them was the crippling space. The sweat was pouring from his forehead. He threw the sweeping-brush to the floor, and pinning his forehead between his hands, he screamed at the dead white walls, "Why, why, why?" It was 'why' that was beyond tears; it was the after-end of sadness, and also its pre-genesis. His 'why' was a complete alphabet of despair. He didn't mind that Ruth had heard him. It didn't matter. He felt a great surge of relief. He had at least asked. Who, what or why, didn't matter. He had made it clear that whatever the question was, he desperately needed an answer. He wanted to know the 'why' of the 'why', and that, at least, was a beginning. He sank into the chair, staring at Ruth without seeing her.

It grew dark outside. Neither of them switched on a light. In the shadow her black loose hair threatened him. He wanted to annihilate her in the blinding night of their bed, and to love her with fury. He took her hand and led her out of the room.

Ruth waited for Jack to undress. Then she switched off the light, shy of him. As she bent her back onto the sheets, her hair fell like an incoming tide over her shoulders. Jack clasped a handful, and kissed it gently onto her back. "Why don't you have your hair cut?" he said. "You know I like it short."

"And I like it long," she answered, "and that's the way I'm going to keep it."

"All right, darling." He put his arms round her. "Grow it as long as you like." He hugged her violently. "As far as I'm concerned," he heard himself saying, "you can trip over it and break your neck."

So it was that they made love.

## 5

Towards the end of their first year together, their partnership seemed to settle, and Ruth ascribed their initial difficulties to the problems of re-orientation. Jack had organized himself in his father's business to the extent that he had more free time which he devoted to his writing. They still quarrelled over trivia but generally they were content, and when monotony threatened, Jack took Ruth to his mother's house to re-fuel. It was a neat and ordered arrangement that could have gone on for ever.

And then Jack's mother fell ill. Suddenly and seriously. The doctors were pessimistic and warned Jack and his father of the inevitable fatal consequence. It was a question of time, and they hoped for everybody's sake that it would not be long. But Jack refused to take them seriously. How could his mother, who in all her life had respected order in all things, whose silver stood ranged on the suburban sideboard in exactly the same order as it had stood in Hamburg, whole letters were neatly filed and answered, who always had stamps, needle and thread, and a phial of aspirin in her handbag, how could she now opt out of his marital arrangement and disrupt it altogether? It was unthinkable. So he visited her even less than was usual, refusing to recognize the change in the status quo.

After a month, Mrs Millar was moved into London, to a

hospital close to Jack's office. For the first week he didn't visit her at all. Occasionally he would telephone and enquire of her health through a nurse. He said he was a friend and made his enquiries as distant as possible. Each day, when his father dropped into the office on his way from the nursing home, Jack made a point of making no reference at all to his mother. He shut his eyes to his father's pallor, and the red blear of sleeplessness over his face. Then one morning when it was over a month that he had not seen her, he found his father waiting for him in his office. He began to unbutton his coat, deliberately refraining from asking his father why he was there. His father stared at him. Both were prepared to outsit the silence in each other. Jack drew up a chair and sat opposite him. He stretched out a hand to play with a pencil on his desk, but quickly withdrew it, because it might have been mistaken as a gesture of communication. Occasionally they stared directly at each other, but most of the time, they stared into the wooden grain on the desk. Jack noticed how the pattern of the wood had been grooved with a pencil. His secretary usually sat there when she took letters. He was suddenly outraged by her wanton destruction and decided as soon as she arrived – she was late anyway – that he would sack her. He was trembling with fury. She had suddenly become the whole cause of the unspeakable agony between himself and his father. He looked up again at the crouched figure opposite him. His father still wore his overcoat and as he shrunk his head into the upturned collar, he uttered a terrible sigh. Jack fidgeted. His father had spoken, and he had to make a gesture of having at least heard. He stared at the grooves on the desk again, and decided that as soon as his secretary arrived, he would kill her. He heard his father get up, and with his eyes, he followed the waist area of his father's coat as it moved towards the door. It was hard enough to keep his eyes down, but to look at his father was impossible. He heard the knob turn on the door.

"She's dying," his father whispered.

Jack heard it in his groin with a sudden spasm of pain. His back shivered as he felt his father suddenly behind him, and he straightened his shoulders to withstand the blow he fully expected his father to land. He felt his father's hand on his head, gentle and caressing, like the touch of a lover. But slowly, with painstaking care, his father gathered a clutch of hair, and tightening his grip, almost plucked it from his scalp. He jerked Jack's head back sharply, so that he was forced to look at him.

"She's dying," he spat at him. "I think you ought to know."

His father had gone from the room, yet he still sat there, his head upturned, his scalp tingling and a stuttering pain in his groin.

"Are you all right, Mr Millar?" He heard his secretary talking. "Can I get you something?"

"Why did you have to draw on the desk?" he said quietly. "Why? Look," he pointed out the grooves. "You spilt it," he said simply. "It was so *nice* before."

He stumbled to get his coat, and blindly found his way to the hospital.

At the entrance, an old man stood, a withered stalk, in the centre of a display of flowers. Jack groped at a bunch of violets.

"Beautiful violets," the old man said, stressing more the name of the flower than its attribute. "But carnations give more of a cheer." Carnations were dear and harder to push. Violets were a curse. They were so cheap and pretty. "Or a couple of chrysanths," he dared. Their price was prohibitive.

But Jack was already handing him the violet money. The old man shrugged his shoulders, and sheathed the bunch in a crumpled piece of tissue. What did it matter, he thought, turning to his next customer, violets, chrysanths or carnations, when death was the same price everywhere.

Jack walked through the corridors of the hospital, postponing enquiries as to the whereabouts of his mother's room. He climbed staircases, and shuffled through halls, storey after storey. Then he found a lift and repeated the same expedition, floor by floor. Until he found himself in out-patients, staring at a huge chromium tea-urn. He sat down on a bench, next to a head-bandaged boy, and stared at the violets that had begun to wither in his hand.

On the far end of the bench sat a young man in a beret. He was reading a French newspaper. A nurse held out her hand towards him.

"Your card, sir."

The man stared at her, uncomprehending.

The nurse caught sight of the newspaper and released a sigh of pity at recognition of his foreign status. For some reason, she thought that the only way of making a foreigner understand was to shout at him. If he couldn't understand English, it could only be because he was deaf.

"Your letter from your doctor," she yelled through the waiting-room.

The man smiled at her, which did not please the nurse at all.

"You can't come here without a letter," she said, loudly and petulantly, enunciating every syllable. "We can't help you without a letter," she announced to the surgery.

The man felt in his inside pocket. The nurse sighed with triumph, and turning to Jack, who looked more English and reliable, she said, "That hit home all right."

The Frenchman raised an eyebrow at this overheard last phrase. He knew the meaning of the individual words, and he had a vision of his own particular "chez-nous" hit with a crowbar. He handed her the letter nervously, and the nurse passed on to Jack.

"Your letter, sir," she said with more confidence.

Jack stared at her. It was not her day.

"A letter," she tried again. "L-E-T-T-E-R." She spelt it out for him patronizingly, as if it were a general rule of the National Health Service to assume that all free patients were illiterate.

Jack got up. "I'm looking for my mother," he had to tell her. "Mrs Millar. She's a private patient. I was just dropping by and I'd like to see her. Not if it's any trouble, of course. I could come back. She'll be coming out tomorrow, anyway. It's just that I want to ask her what clothes I should bring for her to go home in. But if it's any trouble," he begged the nurse to forbid a visit, "I could come tomorrow." He listened to his voice rambling on, as he let himself be led to reception. He heard himself giving details of his mother's name, as if she were a complete stranger. He let himself be guided to her room, where he waited, terrified, outside her door.

The nurse stood by his side, waiting for him to enter and to discharge herself of further responsibility. He heartily wished she would go away and leave him alone. Then with the authority of her position, she raised her red-clenched fist and knocked on his mother's door. Jack heard a feeble 'yes' from inside, a voice too feeble for questioning, only a weak confirmation of presence. He ignored it. He had not asked for entry. He was not ready. What right had this starched, hot-permed, chapped and whiskered dragon to organize his panic.

"Please go away," he said to her.

The dragon frothed slightly, then turned on her dreadfully sensible heel. He was alone, and he knocked gently on the door.

"Yes," the voice stated again. The voice was completely unfamiliar, and as he opened the door and saw her wilting on the bed, he knew that her face too, was that of a complete stranger. He steadied himself towards the bed, aware of the recurring pain in his groin, and as he stretched the violets towards her, he noticed that the grip of his fingers had strangled them.

He saw her lips twitch and she blinked a little. It could have been a look of reproach, but he had to assume it was a smile she was giving him. He sat down beside the bed and wanted to take her hand.

"You'll be out soon, Father says." It sounded ridiculous. He wasn't too sure whether she knew of her condition.

"I know," she mumbled, and he left it there, in the air, not knowing what she was knowing.

"How do you feel?" he tried again, his clenched fist creeping up the counterpane.

"I know it," she said.

"For God's sake," he cried to himself, "don't let me know you know." He looked at her face imploringly. "Let's go on pretending," he advised himself, "like we always have. Like in Germany, when you said it couldn't happen to us. It was only the poor Jews from the East. Like the mezzuzah you made Father take off the front door, like the barmitzvah you wouldn't let me have."

He saw his hand almost touching her white fingers on the bedspread. An inch more and he would touch her. gently, stroke her, caress her, squeeze her, crush her, as his father had stroked, clutched and dragged at his hair.

58

He stared at the white barrier between their two hands.

"Father will take you for a holiday," he said.

"I know," she whispered again.

He didn't understand how anyone, who all her life had lived a lie, should suddenly choose to die in honesty.

"I know I'm dying," he heard her say. He found her hand falling into his.

"You'll get better mother," he said feebly. He wished he could stop crying. His tears were proof of the truth that was now exposed between them.

"I want you to have my gold watch," she said. "I took it for repair to Cooper's. It should be ready on Friday week." She smiled weakly as if her sense of efficiency would guarantee her immortality.

"Your old school reports are in the second drawer of my desk. So is your birth certificate. In the top drawer in an envelope is a lock of your baby hair. The letters you wrote from school are there too. Take them away. They were mine, and will only upset your father. I want no mourning, and a private funeral. Your father will announce it in *The Times*."

She was dying as she had lived, with cold, organized, dignified, inhuman ceremony. She was departing without a fight, without a tear, without a touch of self-pity. He suspected that never in her life had she known real suffering. That sadness had never dwelt in her, and by that token, neither had joy. Such neutrality gave a sense of relief to her dying. She was leaving behind no pain for which he could feel guilty, no sadness for which he could accept responsibility. He had a fleeting feeling that he would quickly forget her.

He lifted her shoulders, cradling her in his arms. He wanted to kiss her, but he kissed her so seldom in his life, it would have sealed the finality of their meeting. He was weeping uncontrollably, the tears falling onto her dry face. He lay her back on the pillows.

"Let me sleep a little," she said.

He made a performance of pulling the sheet away from her face. Her eyes were already closed, and he could see her quick palpitating breathing. The violets lay strewn over the bedspread like a badly embroidered transfer.

"You mustn't die," he whispered. "You can't." She couldn't die before he had learned to accommodate her. She couldn't die and withhold his manhood for ever. He knew he would never see her again, but that all his life, she would possess him.

Outside her door he shivered. He was convinced that just now at his mother's bedside, he had been a ghost in a strange encounter in limbo. He felt a desperate need to relate himself with what was real and true. A nurse was walking down the corridor. Frantically he stretched out his hand towards her, and she supported him as he fell. He managed to look back at the door, and he knew by the excruciating pain in his groin that his mother was gone.


It was many months before Jack's grief mellowed and he was able to take stock of his situation. His mother's death was ill-timed, like a well-loved slipper that wears out before the foot begins to complain, and a slight anger mingled with his sorrow that she had so let him down. His father disturbed him too. His grief was so silent. After a short period of mourning, he went back to his work, and automatically performed the acts of living. Occasionally he would have a meal with Jack after work, but he was always restless and he would leave quickly for home to confront the solid vacuum his wife had left behind. Jack worried about him, but his own pain at his mother's death was still too overwhelming to accommodate pity for his father. Besides, his father's silence angered him. He wanted him to sit before him and weep, loudly and with hot tears, and say, "Look, I'm crying for your mother. That's what my tears are for." But his father grew more silent and pale and his eyes, once bathed in contented wrinkles, now stared out of his head, as if the tears behind them had boiled to saturation and had burned them dry.

Then there was Ruth. She looked after him tenderly, but more and more she became a stranger to him. The vacuum that his mother had left had drawn her further away from him. He found it hard to place her within his life at all. She kept assuring him with her infuriating understanding that he need feel no guilt for his mother's death. But he needed to feel he had had a part in her dying. Ruth would never understand that. By absolving him, she was separating him from part of himself, and he was angry with her at her incursions into his privacy.

But what worried him most of all was his sudden inability to love her. It seemed that when his mother died, all the heart had gone out of his marriage. He was alone with Ruth on an empty stage, with no background to call upon, no wings into which to escape, and above all no audience to censure or applaud his performance. At night he would lie by her side and resent her obvious need of him. Yet he wanted to love her. He had to love her. It was imperative. He wanted to love her as he had loved her in the echoes of his mother's hostility. As time passed, he understood that to do this, he had to replace his third party.

PART TWO

# 6

They say it takes two to make a marriage, but more often it's three, and sometimes four; and acknowledging the reality of his mother's death, Jack Millar turned to affairs.

In his dress business he moved in a woman's world and he didn't have to look far or long. At the time he was organizing his summer collection and preparing the show that would launch it. The agency that supplied him with models was sending him their accessorisor to discuss with him the finishing touches of the display. Jack had arranged for her to come to his office at twelve o'clock. Without realizing it, he was considering the possibility of taking her out to lunch, whoever she might be. When he'd left Ruth that morning, she had seemed to him beautiful. Without make-up and her loose hair, the soap-shine still glistening on her face, he was happy that she was his wife, and he felt an overwhelming sense of freedom, as if a long-standing problem had once and for all been solved, and he could exercise his energies on something else. Towards the middle of the morning he began to get restless, his eye on the clock, wondering how to fill in his time until the accessorisor arrived. Half in earnest, he booked a lunch table for two at a nearby restaurant and he toyed with the idea of getting home very late that night. The idea that the girl would be completely uncompanionable did not occur to him. She was going to be what he wanted, pretty, not too clever and needing his love. She was going to be exactly right for him, and when she arrived, punctually at twelve, he knew, and it is possible that she knew too, and had planned as he had planned, that it would be a late night for both of them.

"My name's Carol," she said, crossing over to the desk to shake his hand.

He smiled. "I'm Mr Millar," he said. He knew at once that she was right for him.

For Carol he was right too. He merely repeated the pattern of her affairs that had begun a long time ago. When she was twenty-five, a good five years ago, her best and loyal girl-friend, with whom she had shared a flat and other things for so long, suddenly opted for the road that Nature had not necessarily intended her to take, and upped and left and got married. And Carol had been punishing her ever since. She was interested only in married men. Over the years, since her friend's betrayal, she had battened off a series of married backs, jumping from one to another with the dexterity of a flea, without pausing for breath between. She preferred the marriages she grazed off to be happy ones, and the wives, like her friend, at least pretty. She had seen Jack before at dress shows, and sometimes his wife was with him. She approved, so that when she met Jack officially for the first time, she was far more consciously prepared than he was. At the time of their meeting, Carol was in a hovering position. Her last affair had been threatened with the loss of wife and children; the host was obliged to arch his back, and Carol to take off. As she walked into Jack's office she made a neat and perfect landing.

She was pretty, as Jack had expected. Everything on her face, including her expert make-up, was in right proportion. But it was a functional face in that each feature fulfilled its prescribed purpose. No more, no less. The eyes were only for seeing, the ears stuck to their hearing. There was no vision on her mouth or sight in her lips. She was nicely and neatly departmentalized and each feature was called upon to do its duty as methodically and coldly as parts of a filing cabinet. She was beautifully dressed, or rather tailored. Two short white cuffs with silver cufflinks, stiff as plaster of Paris, on two broken wrists, were moulded round her long white ringless hands. A tall white starched collar was built around her neck like scaffolding. A black velvet band almost covered her forehead and was fastened in a bow over one ear. The pleats of her grey flannel dress opened gently as she sat down, her feet to the side and together, one hand placed demurely over the other, her eyes lowered over her collar; altogether the picture of a nun on leave.

Jack looked at her and was satisfied. Especially with the cufflinks and the short cropped hair. She was enough of a woman to be proud of, but, unlike Ruth, not enough to represent any kind of challenge to him. He loved her instantly, prepared to forgive in advance all the stupidities and falsities he knew he was bound to find in her. He decided to skip the lunch arrangement, wanting to save himself and his vocabulary until the evening. And Carol, probably with the same thoughts, decided she had to leave for another engagement and fell in with his suggestion that they should discuss the accessories in the evening.

"Shall we have dinner together?" he said.

"It's difficult to lay out all the pictures on a table in a restaurant. Why not come to my flat? I'll give you some supper. I'm not much of a cook, but it'll be something."

The whole speech had the wearied edge of a part in a play that had had a very long run. Her white fingers crawled singly up the scaffolding and touched her chin.

"You'll come?" she said.

"I'll be delighted."

He was slightly disappointed that things had moved so quickly and so easily. Perhaps, later on, he hoped there would be some resistance.

When she had left, he telephoned Ruth. She answered the phone immediately, as if she had been waiting for his call. He put the phone down quickly. He wanted to catch her off guard, to disturb her in the middle of doing something else, so that she wouldn't have time to cross-examine or question him. The idea of her sitting by the telephone, wondering who had replaced the receiver, probably wondering whether it was a woman calling for him made him tremble. He'd better phone again and admit it was he and that the line had been cut. He dialled his number. Again, almost immediately, she replied.

"Hullo darling," he said with forced heartiness. "Yes, it was me," he answered her query. "I heard you say hullo, and then you were cut off. It's probably the new girl on the switchboard." He was startled at his new-found ability to lie, and he went on with greater confidence.

"Look, darling," he said, "I shan't be back till late this evening. A man from Manchester has just phoned. He's in town for the day and I've got to take him out for dinner. No, it's *not* nice, darling. You know how I hate these business dinners. And he's a bore, anyway, or so I'm told. But he's a good customer. No, I don't know where I'll take him," he said carefully. "Haven't got round to that yet. Yes, I know I'm often late, darling. Never mind. We'll make up for it at Christmas. Yes? We'll have a wonderful holiday. Just you and me. Love me?" he said brazenly. "You looked lovely this morning. Yes, wait up for me if you want to, but I may be terribly late. He's going back tonight and I may have to take him to the train. Yes, of course, darling, I'll be back as soon as I can."

"Look after yourself," she said, "and have a good time."

He could have killed her. "It'll probably be hell," he said.

He quickly found the railway timetable he kept on his desk and checked on the time of the last train back to Manchester. 1.30 am. It was a gift. He even began to visualize the fat bowler-hatted bore he would bundle into a sleeper at 1.30 am and then turn wearily away. And what would they have talked about at dinner. Business? No. Only in the beginning. Then they had talked about his hobbies, his outside interests. The man from Manchester wasn't really interested in making money. He wanted to write. Yes, that's right. He wanted to write about himself. His autobiography. No, he wasn't married. His father had died, and he lived with his mother in a rambling house in Manchester. No, his mother was dead too. Absolutely dead. No, he wasn't married. He would never marry. Jack began to like him. He decided he wouldn't make him a fat man. He would be thin, like himself, and without a bowler hat. He was intelligent and a pleasure to be with. Jack took out his pad and began to draw him. He found himself giving the man from Manchester a beard and a bush of black hair. He was tall and elegant, and in his face was a look of detachment from worldly things. Jack liked him more and more. He wondered what he would call him. The man from Manchester deserved a good name. He drew him again. This time he was shorter and without a beard and as Jack trimmed the drawing it became unknowingly more and more of a self portrait. He liked him better. Rallim, he would call him. Rallim from Manchester. Jack's friend. Millar's Rallim. Rallim's Millar. He would see a lot of him. Perhaps even join him for a week-end. His life had become suddenly enriched. He looked at the picture on the pad again and drew a book into the man's hand. He opened his engagement book and wrote the day's entry. Dinner with Rallim from Manchester. 7.30.

The flat was not what he had expected. During the day he had visualized it as large, sparse, with an over-abundance of wood, white walls, an occasional abstract painting, with a room of clinical white tiles that was the kitchen. Instead, it was a doll's house, full of roses. Roses in all shapes and forms, the wall-paper, curtains, rugs, hairbrush, even to the large net rose pinned on to the lavatory cover. It was the flat of a little girl who needed protection, warmth and assurance. At least, that was what Jack was pleased to think. And with a great sense of relief he realized that all that was woman about Carol was expressed in paper plastic and net roses. Had he known the story of the flat and the happiness it had once housed, he would have known that the roses were not Carol at all. They were the contribution of her room-mate, built up over the years, a rose in some form or another to mark each phase in their relationship, a collection which, when she married, she left behind by way of alimony. And Carol had kept them all in their places, hating them, like love-letters from a lost love that one cannot read again but cannot bear to throw away.

She had warned him that she was not a good cook, but Jack hadn't believed her. Again he was wrong. The meal was a tinned one, but served with a delicate finesse. The round mould of salmon that passed as hors d'ouevre was crowned with a rose of parsley. The cold chicken breasts, hemmed in with aspic, retained the shape of the tin, but were garnished each end with petalled tomatoes. The fruit salad at the end of the meal was served in grapefruit cups balanced on a flowered doyley. A pretty meal, which Carol ate prettily with a Swedish no-fork and a rose-covered napkin. When they had finished Jack left the table abominably hungry. He gave a swift nostalgic thought to Mr Rallim from Manchester and the great seven course dinner and conversation they had missed together.

"Now to work," Carol said. "I've got everything ready for you."

The photographs and the accessory samples were spread out on the candlewick roses on the bed. Carol snuggled on the white fur rug and Jack sat down beside her. It was a difficult position to do business in, at least Jack found it so, but Carol seemed not to be handicapped by it. In a business-like fashion she suggested alternative accessories to go with each garment, deftly illustrating them with swift pencilled drawings. From time to time she would ask his opinion, though there was nothing he wanted to dispute. She worked with instinctively good taste and with enormous skill. She immersed herself entirely in the work, becoming in turn each inanimate accessory, a brooch, a necklace, a glove, even a poodle. It was no accident that she was an accessorisor. She herself was a decoration, a luxurious addition. Carol *was* an accessory. Nothing about her was necessary.

She arranged all the ensembles, and put them neatly to one side. The business part of the evening had been accomplished, and it was still only 9.30. Jack was sipping port with Mr Rallim from Manchester. They were daydreaming together of giving up business and living a life devoted to doing the sort of things that made life worth living. Jack was pleasurably bewildered by the sense of how much they had in common.

He found his arm sliding around Carol's neck. He thought for a moment how little they knew about each other, and he wondered whether she was as real as Mr Rallim, or perhaps even if Mr Rallim was as real as she. But even if it were an illusion lying there on the white fur rug, or sipping port in the three-star restaurant, Jack was sure of one thing. He was the object of someone's attention, devotion perhaps, and whatever he was called upon to do he could without any doubt in his mind achieve. He lay beside her and took her hand. She guided it to the lamp switch beside them and turned it off. For himself, Jack didn't need the dark. He knew he needed nothing. Neither the light nor the dark, nor an image nor a sound, nor a dream, nor any kind of evocation. He was there and she was beside him, malleable, responsive, without challenge.

"Here's a toast," he was saying. "To you, Mr Rallim, and to a happy business relationship."

"I hope it won't be confined to business, Mr Millar," Mr Rallim said, raising his glass.

"It's not often one finds someone in this business of ours who's interested in things other than making money," Jack said.

"I've often thought that," Rallim confided. Jack put his hand on Carol's forehead. "Whenever I go into a stock-room and look through the range I wonder, 'What am I doing here? Surely there's more to life than deciding between blues and greens and box or knife pleats. And why do I hate it, and what would I want to do more?'"

"Perhaps," said Jack, "it's a question of status. We all want to succeed in some way or another. We want people to love us, or at least to respect us. Maybe we think we can do it with money. But the trouble with people like us, Rallim, is that we feel there's not much status attached to wealth. No prestige, it's non-creative. We'd rather be writers or painters."

Rallim laughed sheepishly. "I do write," he said timidly. "It's funny but I'm slightly ashamed of it. You're the first person I've ever told." Jack felt the confidence as a milestone in their relationship. He poured some more port into Rallim's glass, in the same way as Carol's flat-mate might have given her another rose. "I'd love to read what you've written," he said.

He unzipped the back of Carol's dress. Never in his life had he felt more full of expectation. This is me, the real Jack Millar, he thought to himself. Until now I have been half alive.

Carol had taken off her scaffolding and placed a cushion under her head. She was concentrating on the image of Jack's wife, evoking a picture of unparalleled beauty. She built around her a white dress, accessorized her and carefully made up her face, using all kinds of tricks to achieve a glowing radiance. As a finishing touch, she planted a smile on her lips, and then she left her, standing on a pedestal, while Carol stepped back to look at her. It was a familiar picture. Carol had lain still on her back and drawn it many times before. And she knew exactly how it would dissolve, yet it never failed to stimulate her. The whiteness of the dress vanished, and the body wilted like a poisoned flower. The bodice parted and bared a wrinkled concave chest. The long neck crêped and the face was drained of its glow. The piled-up blonde hair fell away in patches.

Gradually the whole figure sunk on to its pedestal which itself crumbled into dust. Carol opened her eyes and smiled.

"Why don't you try your hand at writing too?" Rallim said. "There's a lot more to you than making money. You're a man, Millar, a man, man, man."

Jack sank down heavily upon her. He was melting with enormous joy.

"I love you, Carol," he said. "I love you."

And he decided to have dinner with Mr Rallim again as soon as possible.

When he got home at two o'clock, the hall lights were out and he went quietly to the bedroom. Ruth was sitting up in bed reading. He was startled to see her there. And for the first time since he'd spoken to Mr Rallim he realized that he was married and that the woman in the bed was his wife.

# 7

It was not long before Ruth began to notice that Jack's dress business which legitimately took him out of town two days a month, now made extra demands on him and he was away sometimes for a whole week. At about the same time he had increased her housekeeping money.

"Buy yourself something," he would say under his breath and sneak out of the front door to work.

Alone in the house, she would try to drown the suspicions that nagged at her. She would try to legitimize his absences. It was the busy season. He was working hard; he was working for her, and momentarily she cursed herself for being so ungrateful.

But the season was not that busy. Last year at this time, he had been home more often. It was true his business was expanding. Did he not, every day over breakfast, regale her with the increase in turnover? "If we go on like this," he would say, "we'll go public in five years." Sometimes it was three years, sometimes only one. He insisted on the topic every morning, as if increase in turnover would justify his behaviour. It was a conversational point beyond her understanding, or her interest, but he laboured at it, offering her a new connection between them. He talked to her of little else but the business. Like two strangers they met at the table, and like two strangers they touched each other at night. It was true that he was loving her again, but with an abandon that was completely alien to his nature. Jack was not basically a happy man, and it was this sudden quality of happiness in his behaviour that Ruth found most suspect of all.

"Yes," she convinced herself, "he has another woman."

At such moments, she would make a sudden decision to leave him. She would pack a case, praying that her determination would not desert her. But before strapping it down, she had gratefully talked herself into believing that her suspicions were groundless. "He's working overtime," she would say to herself. "He's doing it for me."

But as she cleared the breakfast table that morning, she heard again the light-heartedness of his parting words. "Late again tonight, darling. Don't wait up for me."

She slammed the dishes back on to the table. She felt a need to do something dramatic. She had in some way to call attention to herself. Should she go, and leave him a note? But that was not sudden enough. Not sufficiently irrevocable. If she were to leave him, she had to do it while he was in the house, so at least she could be begged to remain. She screamed aloud into the empty kitchen. There must be something she could do. If only she'd thought of it earlier, she could have put her head in the gas-oven, while he was still in the house and could save her. She shuddered at the thought. It wasn't for her, the gas-oven. Suicide was a waste of a good death. You only had one, and you should make the most of it.

She would phone him at the office. Yes, that's what she would do. She would tell him she knew about the affair. She would not be prepared to argue with him or to accept any of his lies. She would simply state with dignity that she was leaving him. She clenched her teeth and dialled the number.

He answered the phone himself, and his voice paralysed her. "What is it, darling?"

"I . . . er . . . I was just thinking," and she did just that, very quickly. "I . . . Did you say this morning the turnover was ten thousand or twenty?" She heard herself laughing. "I just thought twenty was a bit fantastic," she dragged on.

"But it's right," he said, "and next year we'll double."

"That's wonderful."

"Be good." She saw him smiling. "I must ring off. A client's just arrived."

As she put the phone down, she noticed she was crying. She had connived in his own manoeuvring. She didn't give a damn what the turnover was. She wouldn't be fobbed off with his increases. His heartiness on the phone terrified her. Tonight, when he came home, she would confront him. It was the least she could do, and probably the most. Yet she hoped desperately that whatever the truth, he would deny it. How could she accommodate his admission? She would have to leave him, and she knew how impossible such a move would be. She sat at the kitchen table and stared ahead of her. For some unknown reason, she began to wonder what she was wearing. She tried to recollect how she had dressed that morning, but without looking at herself she had no idea. She looked down at her body and acknowledged her terrible coverings. The grey skirt, the black stockings, the black pullover, the ensemble in fact, she had worn night and day for the past three weeks. The clothes that had come in on her pain, and had stayed with her in familiar loyalty.

She sniffed about herself. "I smell," she said to the kitchen wall, and it gave her a quaint sense of security.

That evening when he came home from work, again very late, she asked him where he had been.

"I've been having a drink with a client."

"What's his name?" she asked as disinterestedly as possible.

There was an undeniable hesitation.

"Mr . . . um . . . Rallim." His stammering still echoed in the pause that Ruth allowed before questioning him further.

"You don't seem too sure," she said with contempt.

"What d'you mean?" he shouted at her with unwarranted anger.

"You seem to be seeing a great deal of Mr Rallim nowadays," Ruth went on calmly.

"What if I am? Who's going to run the business? Do you bring any money into the house?"

He was anxious to reverse their positions and become himself the accuser.

"Mr Rallim must greatly increase your turnover," Ruth held on to her position.

"It so happens he does."

"Or is it *Miss* Rallim?" Ruth stared at him and watched him grow pale.

He didn't answer.

"I want to know," she insisted.

It was easier to tell her than to keep it a secret much longer. In any case, the only drawback to his relationship with Carol was his inability to share his happiness with anybody else. And it was Ruth above all he wanted to share it with as he had shared with her his agony and love for his mother. Perhaps she and Carol might even become friends. Close friends. Ruth would be understanding enough for that.

"Well?" Ruth sat down. Her tone of voice had changed as if she expected the worst and was prepared to come to terms with it.

"Yes," Jack said, almost eagerly. "It is." He fully expected Ruth to congratulate him.

Ruth stood up. She was calm, although she was trembling.

"D'you want a divorce?" she said evenly.

Jack shuddered. The idea had never for one moment occurred to him.

"You're mad," he whispered.

Ruth was furious at his arrogant diagnosis.

"What do you expect me to do? Have her over to dinner? Make her a bosom pal? Tuck you both in perhaps?"

Yes, that was what he wanted. Exactly that. He couldn't see what was so very wrong with it. He couldn't understand, if Ruth loved him, as she claimed to do, why she wasn't interested in his happiness.

"It's not as important as all that," he backed out weakly.

"D'you want to marry her?" Ruth insisted.

The shock of his confession was beginning to grip her in its reality. She wanted to know who the girl was, how she walked, smiled and dressed, the details of her face, so that she could obliterate every particle of her. But she was too proud to reveal any interest in his choice.

Jack began to laugh and it infuriated her.

"You make it sound so serious," he said. "Marry her. I've had my lesson with you," he teased, going up to her and stroking her hair.

"Don't touch me," Ruth shouted at him. "Your hands are dirty."

"That kind of talk won't get you anywhere," he said angrily.

"What right have you to be angry with me?" she said.

She tried to hold back her tears in case he would mistake them for a weapon. But he saw them welling on her eyelids.

"Don't cry," he said gently, "please don't cry. It'll be all right. I promise. It'll blow over. Just give me time. Please give me time. It's not important," he said, trying to convince himself. "We'll be all right, I promise you."

"Will you really try?" she said pleadingly, hating herself for not denying him.

"Of course."

He was overjoyed at her acceptance, and she shivered as he kissed her.

"It'll be all right," he said again, but he meant it not for her but for himself.

For the first few weeks after the discovery, Jack came home from work early, and Ruth began to believe that it was all over. But once he had convinced her, Jack took the risk of lying again. Instead of lunching with Mr Rallim he began to dine with him. Each night he would come home late and be furious to find Ruth waiting up for him. Often she would anticipate his excuses, offering them to him when he came home. A traffic jam or seasonal overwork, and he would agree gratefully. She accepted his lies because, had she refused to believe him she would have been obliged, out of self-respect, to leave him. But one night after a succession of late dinners she questioned him gently.

"Jack, are you sure it was Mr Rallim again?"

"No, it wasn't," he said. Her feigned belief over the past few weeks had been a strain on him too, and it was a relief to have the truth between them. At the sign of her tears he said once again:

"Please give me time, Ruth. In any case," he said, suddenly inspired, "I can't just drop her like that. It's not fair. I've got to do it gently." He thought it was a brilliant move.

"The longer you leave it, the harder it will be," Ruth said coldly. She was unimpressed by his sudden sense of responsibility.

"I'll try," he said helplessly. "It'll be all right, you and me. I promise you. Just give me time. Please give me time."

He was home early for a few nights after that, but the intervals of fidelity became shorter and shorter. Ruth was weary of giving him time. He seemed to be needing an eternity. Often she thought of compelling him to choose between them, but she shrank from the idea. It would be pointless. She understood that Miss Rallim had become an essential part of their marriage. Who she was or how she looked was irrelevant. If it were not Miss Rallim it would be somebody else. She knew that as long as she acquiesced, Jack would make no move to put an end to the affair. In fact she was as essential a part in the relationship as the girl herself; she at home, waiting, loving, and hoping, created the tension for Jack's side-affair. Without her, the affair would evaporate.

She was horrified at her conclusion. If this were true, she was trapped. Again she decided to leave him, and again she packed a case, but there was no-one in the house to beg her for more time.

Now she was often alone. She sat in front of the gas-fire, watching the heat tattoo her legs a mottled red, sitting always on the edge of the same chair, staring always at the same tile on the fireplace. Each time he came home late, she began, against her better judgement, to nag him, to check on his movements, to torture herself with confirmation of what she already knew.

"Give me time," he would say, continually, until the phrase was an obscenity.

"How can you use me like this?" she screamed at him. "Or is it her you are using? It's breaking us up," she said quietly. "We can't be alone together any more. Your functioning depends on my humiliation."

She shouldn't have said it. He couldn't bear her understanding. With her logic she had diminished him. She had shown him to be what he feared he was, a frightened man, uncommittable, cruel, selfish, vain. How could she she stay with him and bear the duplicity and understand it at the same time.

"But I do love you," he said bewildered. "I do." He tried to say her name, but he daren't relate the hurt he was causing to the woman he loved and had married.

He went over to her and stroked a panel of hair that had fallen across her face.

"I'm sorry," he said. His voice sounded automatic.

"What are you sorry for?" Ruth was going to make an issue of it.

"I'm just sorry."

"Yes, but what for?" she insisted. She was at her understanding again.

"I'm sorry. Isn't that enough?" He could feel his throat taut. "I'm sorry," he shouted, "and I don't damn well know what I'm sorry for. I'm sorry about hurting you, I'm sorry I love you, I'm sorry you should love me, I'm sorry I married you, I'm sorry for every damn thing I've never been or done." He sat on the bed, his head drooping. "I'm just sorry," he whispered.

Ruth pulled him towards her and cradled him in her arms.

"God help me," she whispered, "but I love you."

"Give me time," he begged, "It'll be all right, I promise you."

# 8

Over the months, Jack increased her housekeeping allowance and sneaked out of the front door more quickly. He found it more and more difficult to conceal his irritation and above all, his fury at her misery. She was becoming slip-shod in her dress as well, making herself ugly, to gain, he supposed, his pity. He respected her too much ever to feel sorry for her, but her unhappiness moved him unbearably. He had often wondered how he could compensate her, but to offer her anything short of his love was an admission of his nagging guilt. He tapped his inside pocket. It was a gesture he had often made over the past few weeks. Inside was a gift for her, but since the day he had acquired it, there had never been a right moment to hand it over. Since his affair with Carol, and as long as it would last, he knew that there was not, and never would be a right moment. He would have to wait till the affair was done with, when a present no longer looked like a premium. He was doubtful about the gift anyway. It wasn't exactly genuine. It was really a gift to him from his father, who, to mark his son's twenty-first birthday, had bought Jack a number of shares in a South African gold-mining company. Today, they were worth a considerable sum, and for tax purposes Jack found it advisable to transfer the shares to Ruth's name. It was all a bit of a cheat, really. But he had to give them to her sooner or later. There was a regular correspondence from the company, and now it would come addressed to her. It would look far more like hush-money if she had news of the gift from another source. He tapped his pocket again in postponement and she saw the gesture as she brought in the coffee. "Are you hiding something?" she said. "I mean, is there anything else you're hiding?"

He fought down his irritation. "I've got something for you," he said. It came out of his mouth when he wasn't looking. He heard the words, and he wondered what he could do with them. He couldn't pick them up and hide them again. They were too obviously exposed, demanding some clarification. "I've got something for you," he said again, as if to test his voice for its reality.

"I heard," she said coldly.

"Don't you want to know what it is? It's a present."

She went up to him and he took the envelope out of his pocket. The presentation had to be casual, and he attempted an off-hand manner, but with all the explanations that had to accompany the gift, how was it possible to be casual. A shrug of the shoulder lasted a second, the time it took to throw a diamond necklace onto the table and to say, "That's for you." There it would lie, brightly and amply speaking for itself. But how could he shrug his way through the story of his father's gift to him, his transfer of the gift to her, what the shares were worth, and so on and so on, without shrugging himself into a cripple. He took a deep breath, and told her the whole story, holding the envelope in his hand. "When I was twenty-one," he began, and there seemed no end to the weary tale he had to tell. As it unwound itself, it revealed how undeniably manoeuvred the gift had been, so that he wanted to take it back and apologize for having tried to pull a fast one on her.

She listened until he was done, when, with a belated, and now rather pointless gesture of disregard, he flung the envelope onto the table.

Ruth stared at it for a long time, before turning to him. "I want a baby," she said.

He fully expected the gift to be dismissed but her infallible interpretation of its superficiality infuriated him. "Don't crowd me," he said. "Don't press me. Give me time. I'm not ready."

"But I am ready," she said, and it sounded like indecent exposure.

"We'll start a family in time," he hedged, and Ruth realized that you need two people to make a baby. Two people is the minimum. It is also the maximum.

In order to accommodate her unhappiness, she subconsciously split herself into two. She syphoned off part of herself to feel and absorb the pain, while she allowed the other part of her to manipulate it. To this latter part she delegated desperate activity. Crossword puzzles, horoscope readings, competition entries and visits to fortune-tellers; all were attempts to find a possible solution to a situation which in itself seemed insoluble. The two fortune tellers she visited did not see eye to eye. One forecast a trip overseas in the very near future; the other could see no journey at all. One saw an issue of six children, but the other sadly scraped along a barren line. But on one point, they were both in agreement.

"Don't worry, my dear," they said, "I know it's hard sometimes to believe, but your man really loves you."

It was a statement applicable to any married woman desperate enough to visit a fortune-teller.

She bought magazines concerned with prediction, and in the back page of one of these she found a small advertisement. "Aba ben Saal," it read, "will read your future."

She was impressed by the blandness of it and the complete lack of references that adorned all similar advertisements. Aba ben Saal had not been consulted by sundry duchesses of the realm, neither had kings not made a move without his sanction. Nobody swore by his prophecies, and everybody, it seemed, could move a step without him. All he had was a name and a telephone number.

"May I make an appointment?" Ruth found it difficult to disguise her voice.

"When can you come?" The man's voice was devoid of invitation.

"Can I come now?"

"What is your name, please?"

"Does that matter?" Ruth said, playing for time.

"Madam, I have many clients. If you do not want to tell me who you are, give me any name at all, and stick to it, so that I can record an appointment in my book."

"Mrs Nash," she said.

He opened the door himself and led her into a small study at the back of the house. There was little of the east about Aba ben Saal. He was tall and fair, with an offputting dimple in one cheek, that seemed to resent not having an opposite number. His hair was inclined to curl and he had attempted to iron it with grease, but it was a losing battle. He wore a tweed hacking jacket and suede shoes. He was no more Aba ben Saal than Ruth was Mrs Nash, and they sat at the table together in their accepted deceit of each other.

"Shall I have something of yours to hold?" he said.

She gave him her purse, and the moment he took it, she felt a sense of loss, of her will deserting her, as if he had prepared her to believe everything he was to say.

"You've had a rough time," he began.

"Yes," she agreed eagerly. "It hasn't been easy."

He shivered suddenly. "I see your husband with papers. Lots of papers. He is, I think, a printer." He paused, making a note of her lack of reaction, and quickly he amended his diagnosis. "He has much to do with papers. A journalist he is, or a writer."

"That's right," Ruth pounced on him. She was anxious for the man's success.

"He is a very good writer," the man went on, and Ruth could have hugged him.

"I see a journey very soon, and on the journey, your husband is playing chess." He shuddered. "Now it is very dark," he said, "it's not death-dark. It is sad-dark. After the chess, there is sadness."

He shivered back into his chair and asked for her hand. "In a year or two, you will find happiness. Great happiness," he said, "and it will be with your present husband."

At this latest prediction, she had already forgotten his prophecy of sadness. Whatever it was, it would be overcome. She was going to be happy, and it would be a happiness with Jack. Silently she forgave him for all the past hurt; she would endure the transition into the happiness Aba ben Saal promised her.

He dropped her hand and shivered again. "I see a woman with a ladle in her hand. She is never without the ladle. She is proud of you, but she worries about your marriage. Your father has passed on. He wears a skull cap and is watching you."

"My grandfather." Ruth didn't want to fault him, but she felt it unfair to her father if she did not correct him on that score. "My father's alive," she said. "It was my grandfather who wore a skull cap. It is he who has died."

"Your grandfather," Aba droned on. What was a generation or two between friends. "I see him with a meat-axe. He was a butcher."

Aba was way out, and Ruth began to feel sorry for him. She wanted to help him along, to give him a crib to her life. She began to feel responsible for his failure. "Yes, he was a butcher," she lied remembering his long tailoring bench, where as a child she had played with his chalks and buttons.

"I see him in a shop and you are helping to wrap up the meat," Aba went on, encouraged.

"Yes," she agreed heartily. Perhaps it was the other Ruth he was talking about, the one who was manipulating her own pain.

Aba took her hand again. "I told you about your journey," he said. "This journey is of great importance. I see you alone in a far country and the sad-dark is around you too."

He stared at her as if seeing her for the first time, and he handed her back her purse as a sign that his prophesies had run dry. Ruth gave him his fee which he dropped into a caddy on the mantelpiece. He bowed her politely out of the room, and though he stared at her as she left, Ruth had the feeling he would never recognize her again. The visit depressed her. She eagerly accepted his prediction of her happiness, and she tried to dismiss his more ominous forecasts. He had been wildly off the track with her grandfather. But the occasional streaks of uncanny truth in his reading nagged her for a long time.

She decided that the active Ruth should give up prediction, so she set her to entering competitions. She sent in twelve attempts at listing the important features of a dream house. Central heating in each entry stood high on the list and she picked out parquet flooring, double glazed windows, and pastel shades with a pin. Cellar space inevitably ranked low in each entry, until, dazed by the sundry modern conveniences of the house, the desperate organization of each corner, the sickening egg-shell paints, she decided that one had to have somewhere to get away from it all and hide. In her last entry, the cellar took first place.

She competed in like manner for a mink coat, a mini-car, and a life pension. She bought newspapers greedily for the back-page crosswords and the centre-spread quizzes. She tested herself on whether she had the equipment for fame, or whether she was a good wife, scoring five as a maximum for each question. She allowed the press analysts to decide whether she had charm, was domineering, or would qualify as Prime Minister. And when she ran out of quizzes, she did them again on behalf of Jack, and she worried that her scorings were higher. But when the quizzes were over, and the crosswords complete, when the competition entries were posted and the horoscopes had been combed, the sheer fact of loneliness could no longer be postponed. It was then that Ruth became herself, that the feeler of the pain would merge with its manoeuvrer, and the agony of the equation was unbearable.

She dreaded the nights most of all. Though she never ceased to want him, the machinery of his love offended her. Once or twice he had called her Carol, and she wondered how she could still desire him. She had accepted the situation, but it had not lessened the pain. She received his late nights with sad and stubborn silence, and as he delivered greater hurt, the threshold of her acceptance increased.

After one dinner with Mr Rallim, he crept home quietly at eight o'clock in the morning, Ruth heard his key in the door, and his painstaking sock-steps in the hall. She waited for him to open the bedroom door, but she heard him pass and go into the bathroom. Then, in horror, she heard him drawing a bath. In her cold, frightened body, she knew what he was doing. She waited. He was taking the leisured time of an innocent. Eventually she noticed the bedroom door handle turn slowly and softly, and it revolved around her heart like a saw.

Seeing her sitting up in bed, positively waiting, confused and frightened him. He opened his mouth stupidly and half smiled.

"Why can't you use *her* bathroom for your ablutions?" Her voice had a strange innocent ring that surprised her.

Jack laughed. He didn't mean to laugh. It was his embarrassment and his distress that had to release something. He felt the bedside lamp breeze by his head, and it shattered on the door behind him. For some reason, he felt relieved.

"It's not enough to inflict pain," she said bitterly, "you have to be around to witness it too."

He knew she was right, but he had to defend himself. He could not admit to such monstrous behaviour. "It's not true," he said weakly, "It just isn't true." He crossed over to the bed and Ruth prayed that she wouldn't want him.

"I love you," he said. "That's all that matters, isn't it. I'm still here. I haven't left. Give me time," he whispered. He stroked the back of her hair and said, as he had said so often as a prelude to a new beginning, "We must stay together. I know it's right for us. I love you. That's why it's right."

He took her in his arms, and in a solid hangover of Carol, he loved her with fury and intense joy.


That evening, he suggested they go out for dinner together. He arranged to pick Ruth up from the office. When he left her in the morning, he made an honest resolution to himself to give up Carol. He had to try with Ruth alone. He wanted it to succeed more than anything. In any case, Carol had told him that she would be out of town for a week. It would give him a chance. The resolution became stronger as he neared his office, and when he arrived, he rang Ruth to tell her he loved her. Ruth had a talent for forgiveness that was as sudden as it was absolute and immediately all the agony of the past months evaporated. She bought a new dress to celebrate their coming together, and when he arrived in the evening to fetch her, it would have been difficult not to find her almost beautiful.

"Are you ready?" Jack said.

She heard a tinge of irritation in his voice. "I'll just get my coat." He did not help her into the car, but sat waiting at the wheel for her to settle. They drove through the suburb in silence. Ruth looked at him, begging for some compliment, but he stared ahead of him as if unaware of her presence. She took her compact out of her bag and repowdered her adequately powdered nose. "Do I look all right?" her voice was almost frightened.

He smiled without looking at her. "You look beautiful," he said.

"Why can't you tell me then?" she screamed at him. "Why do I have to ask?"

He patted her knee gently. He thought of Carol and the coming week without her, and he decided to take Ruth to Carol's favourite restaurant.

It was a Chinese restaurant near the London docks. They sat down and studied the menu. The lavish spread on the next table to theirs, bristling with prawns, pineapple and mushrooms, ablaze in reds, greens and browns, made them envious and when their own food arrived it seemed meagre and dull by comparison. The grass in someone else's garden is always greener especially in a Chinese restaurant on your neighbour's table. They picked up their chopsticks as professionally and as casually as possible, gripping them like a vice, not daring to let up on their conversation in case one of them thought the other was having difficulty. They were discussing Jack's approaching holiday and what they would do with the month he was taking off. Jack picked up a piece of Ruth's chicken with a dexterity that astonished him. He poised it in mid-air, daring it to fall off, and as he put it into his opened mouth he swallowed noisily and turned pale, gaping at the couple who had come in through the door. Carol. But who was the man she was with? Ruth followed his gaze. "What a beautiful girl," she said enthusiastically and as she looked at Jack she saw a single red vein sprout from his forehead, a sign of anger or fever, or both. Until she saw Jack's reaction and understood what it meant she hadn't realized how off-key her remark had been, rather like a violinist who doesn't realize he's playing out of tune until he lands on an open string. Jack was either unable or indifferent to concealing his embarrassment. He dropped his chopsticks and the piece of chicken fell obligingly back into the dish.

"Miss Rallim?" Ruth ventured. She had not imagined her so beautiful. But Jack was not concerned with establishing her identity. Who was the other man? What right had she to be with him? She had lied to him. He was wincing with jealousy and bitterness at the deception. He finished his meal without appetite. Ruth too was unnerved. She was anxious to get the meal over with. Both swore to each other they couldn't touch a dessert, and they left the restaurant quickly and disheartened. On the way home in the car, they sat very close to each other. Neither of them spoke. Ruth was half aware of her minor triumph but she was more engrossed and bewildered by her concern for his hurt.

When they reached home, he put his arm around her. "Ruth," he said, and that was all. He had called her by her name, and it expressed his acceptance of the inevitable fact that they were now together and alone.

Over the next few weeks, he was not surprised that desire had drained out of his body. Now he did not touch her at all, and Ruth was terrified of complete dissolution. She began to beg him, and he could not bear her self-imposed humiliation.

"I can't," he said, infuriated by her pain. "Don't you understand?" he shouted at her. "My mother's dead."

"And for the record," Ruth reminded him. "Miss Rallim isn't playing any more."

He crumbled at the stark truth of it. "Have patience," he begged. "Give me time." He thought of the present of the gold-mine shares. Now would have been an honest moment to have given them to her. But the truth had come out of the blue, like a sudden spectre, and there was nothing at hand to honour it.

## 9

She tried to have patience but she feared his neglect of her was damaging. She was told so often that she was not wanted, she began to be convinced of her undesirability. He never touched her, and she began to suspect she was untouchable. And she decided, coldly and deliberately, after months of neglect to put herself to the test.

She met Frank in a coffee-bar. His set up was tailor-made. He worked at night as a waiter, but during the day he painted at home in his flat overlooking Primrose Hill. Ruth didn't enter the relationship easily. To give her her due, she had a struggle. She half wanted him, and in the wanting she already felt committed, already disloyal. The act itself would be a mere formality. But as their coming together became more and more inevitable, her appetite for Frank crumbled. But she went to him nonetheless, to his room overlooking Primrose Hill. She didn't want him and to punish herself she would have him.

The house had a panel of speaker-bells down one side of the front door. Seven bells in all and each serving three tenants. A landlord's gold mine. She rang the bell marked Woodfield three times. Almost immediately a high-voltage voice, as if laced by a short circuit, crackled, "Who's there?"

Ruth was shocked into the necessity of having to reveal her identity. She couldn't just say "It's Ruth." It was like saying "I've come to you. I'm guilty." She hesitated. "It's me," she said. She couldn't commit herself further.

But Frank wasn't going to make it easy for her. "Who's me?" the voice throbbed.

"It's me," she said again, as if the repetition would identify her.

Again the throbbing, "But who's me?"

Ruth wanted to go home. "It's me," she said miserably, "the girl you met in the coffee-bar." She removed the event from herself as far as possible. She felt like a pick-up.

"For God's sake," the voice discharged. "I meet thousands of girls in coffee-bars. What's your name?"

"Ruth." It was out. She hated him. After all, even at confession you are not expected to give your name. "It's Ruth," she shouted again. It's me, she thought. It's me, selling myself through a public microphone like a call-girl. It's my body, lodging in my skin. It's the body of Ruth Millar, née Lazarus, bespoken to Jack Millar, tender Jack Millar, gentle, small-eared, black hair on back of hands. . . . She turned to go away from the door.

"Push," the voice said.

Automatically she turned again, and went into the house, with a numb hatred of everything she stood for.

His room was dark. A great sheet of red hessian was slung across the window hooked on each side by two large safety pins. It was a room that overlooked Primrose Hill pointlessly. Beneath the window was the bed, newly made, the sheets fairly shrieking with whiteness. Frank was sitting on a rocking chair by the gas fire. He was listening to a record of an American folk song. Ruth glanced at the gramophone and noticed that the record had just been put on, probably at the moment he had remotely opened the front door.

"Marvellous, marvellous," he said. "Sit down and listen.

God, what a voice. I could listen to her for hours. I do," he laughed. "God, what a woman. She's got earth in her larynx. Listen to that tremolo."

"I'd like to," said Ruth, sitting down, "if you'd only let me."

"Sorry," he laughed, "I'll shut up. It's just that I love that woman. Look at that face." He picked up the record sleeve from the floor. "Black as night, and everybody's mother." Ruth dutifully looked at the picture, found nothing extraordinary in the face, and turned the sleeve over to read the copy.

"Read it afterwards," Frank said impatiently. "Listen, can't you. It's great. And the one after this is even better."

It was a long playing record and Ruth viewed the prospect dismally. And maybe he'd insist on the other side too. The voice grated on her nerves. She tried to pretend enthusiasm, staring intently at the record player, as if a recording were a visual form of entertainment. Frank prattled on, extolling the virtues of the various interpretations and how every other folk singer was pale beside her.

"She's the queen of them all," he kept saying. "I'll play you another version of this song, and I won't tell you who the singer is. You'll be surprised."

Ruth sat up straight in her chair, dutifully preparing herself to be surprised.

"I've got a helluva collection," he went on, the poor singer struggling to be heard in the background, "but this is my favourite. God, what a voice." Ruth wondered whether he'd ever sat alone and listened to it.

"What do you think of my record?" he asked, rocking in his chair. He was like all collectors. He gave the impression that he had personally composed the music, sung the song, accompanied it on every instrument in the band,

and technically recorded it. If Ruth had told him what she thought of his lousy record he would have taken it as a personal affront. She was silent and whiled away the time examining his room. A three-quarter partition at one end shut off the kitchen, or probably a kitchen with a bath, because the flue of a large geyser was visible on the top of the wall. A large tea-cloth, on which was written a recipe for coq au vin was pinned on the kitchen door. Frank was a 'right' person. He had the 'right things'. A string of French onions and garlic was also visible through the door. 'Right.' A bamboo partition came out of the fireplace at a tangent, and in the intervals of the canes there were rubber plants, and coloured abstract glass pieces. Another collection. Frank simply couldn't do anything wrong. A guitar hung on the wall, with coloured ribbons draped from the neck. A stuffed parrot in a Victorian glass case seemed to Ruth to be indispensible to the folk-song cult. The glossies lay on the table and not a single hard-backed book in sight. A *Guide Michelin* was pointedly visible on the mantelpiece. Ruth visualized Frank's car. On the back window there were surely vulgar coloured proofs of his flying visits to Monaco, Cannes, Nice, Spain, Greece, etc. Frank had been everywhere, to all the right places. Oh, yes. Frank was a 'right' person all right. He made her sick. She stared again at the gramophone and the ugly voice that was still trying to make itself heard against Frank's continual chatter. At last, the record came to an end. Frank got up and for one moment Ruth dreaded that he might be turning it over. But he stopped the machine and took the record off.

"I didn't think you'd come," he said.

"Why not?"

"I thought you might prefer the idea of it to the actual performance."

"I was curious."

"About what?"

"How you live," Ruth said limply.

"Well, this is it. You've seen it. A bed, a few chairs, and a hungry gas fire. Very hungry." Ruth had an unaccountable feeling that he was asking her for shillings. "An easel, some paints," he went on, "and a one-man show of unfinished pictures. Surely you came for some other reason."

"You're not making it easy for me," she said.

He came towards her, putting his arms on her shoulders. "I just want you to be sure of what you're doing," he said. He slid her coat off and led her towards the bed. "After all," he said, "you've more to lose than I." Ruth allowed herself to be led, even co-operating with him, moving a chair which interrupted their direct route to the bed. She knew that the sheets were not always clean like that. That they would lie on the bed for the duration of their affair, however long it might last. Frank had made his only gesture. He had changed his sheets, as he would change them again when another Ruth came along. She threw the covers back and sat down limply on the bed. Frank stood back to look at her. It was her cue to start applying the mystique which she had brought with her as separately as her handkerchief. Slowly she began to undress. She unbuttoned her blouse, gently, and with intermittent shows of modesty. She took it off in shy spasmodic movements, putting up vain attempts at self-resistance, which was difficult considering she was doing it all on her own. Frank stood there, looking at her, not even intently, but seeing her because she happened to be in his line of vision. She had begun to hate him, and to savour the humiliation he was subjecting her to. She hoped she would hate him always; she hoped that she could never enjoy him. She daren't allow herself any pleasure. She looked down at herself, and found with some surprise that she was naked. She was relieved that she felt no shame, that there was nothing in the whole room or in the person who stood in front of her that was in anyway associated or comparable with the man whom, God help her, she loved and wanted and was lonely for. Frank continued to look at her, and Ruth got up and turned around, slowly and casually, like an unconcerned mannequin who could neither profit nor lose by a sale. Then shrugging her shoulders she got into bed.

"What sort of dreams d'you have?" Frank asked with sudden earnestness as if he really wanted to know, as if he had prepared a long one-sided conversation on dreams and character, which he no doubt delivered to each consumer of clean sheets.

"I don't dream."

"Then you have no imagination."

Ruth sat up in bed. It was a position that did not flatter her but momentarily she was indifferent to the mystique.

"Listen," she said, slightly angry. "I've come here. Isn't that enough? Must we have vocabulary between us too? I don't want a relationship with you. I don't want to come close to you. I want connection. Just that. Connection."

Frank stood looking at her but he made no move towards the bed. Ruth turned away from him, her face averted. Almost immediately she heard Frank move. She heard the speed of his undressing and she knew that she must not look at him. Soon she felt him beside her and she turned towards him. She noticed that his eyes were closed, probably in the childlike belief that he was invisible. She lay on her back and over his shoulder once more studied the lay-out of his room.

On the mantelpiece various people were 'At Home' or

had been 'At Home' as some time or another to Frank Woodfield. Ranged against the wall in casual order for her benefit, it was clear that Frank Woodfield was socially in demand, in the past, where the invitations had curled slightly with age, as well as in the future. On the opposite wall hung some of his pictures, all boldly signed, which was the only indication that they had been finished. Ruth had seen them all before, over and over again in the dozens of mushroom galleries throughout London. Then on the bed-side table she caught sight of something that Frank had overlooked in his preparations. A small piece of paper, on which was written, "Memo. David Little owes me 3/5½d." Ruth found meanness in a man unpardonable. The realization that she found herself in such a position with such a man would normally have offended her. But her growing dislike of Frank amused her. There was something so ridiculous in their complete incompatibility. She shifted herself a little, because his weight and movements discomforted her. She was completely detached from the whole performance, which she viewed with the matter-of-factness and the boredom of a whore. Over in the corner opposite the bed was the sink. A wide range of toilet articles was distributed across a glass shelf. A terribly pink towel was folded in immaculate pleats over a towel rail and sadly and alone proclaimed in blue embroidery that it was HIS. The whole ablution corner was ordered with almost homosexual fastidiousness. She was forced for a moment to look at the head that rested below her chin, and she smoothed it tenderly with her hand. On the floor beside the sink were four pairs of highly-polished shoes, each shoe stuffed with a shoe-tree. It was like the joke corner in a shop. The idea that she could be made love to by a man who not only displayed old invitations, made notes of paltry debts, used

HIS towels, and to cap everything kept trees in his shoes, hurt her so much that she began to laugh. Quietly at first and then with a sort of hysteria. Frank seemed not to hear her laughter. He was obviously as detached from the performance as she was. He was only working the act; he had no stake in the production. She took his head in both hands and with all the hatred, contempt and disgust for his pathetic folk-song cult, his neatness and his meanness, she whispered, "I love you, Frank, I love you." It was the least she could have said.

She manoeuvred herself slowly off the bed, and Frank made no move to keep her. She dressed quickly to cover up the feeling of self-disgust that seemed to be drowning her. She looked down at her body and had never found it so ugly. And she knew at the same time that she would come again tomorrow, and the next day, hating it more and more.

"Will you come tomorrow?" he asked from the bed. It was also the least he could say.

"I'll see."

"You'll come," he said. "I know you will."

Why was it taking her so long to dress. Each suspender had to be untwisted. Her blouse seemed suddenly too tight for her, and the zip of her skirt stuck. She threw her coat over her half-dressed state, desperate to get out of the room and to be Ruth again.

"I'm going," she said as she reached the door.

"I'll see you tomorrow," Frank said sleepily.

"Perhaps."

"Come a bit later," he said. "I want to do some work."

"I doubt whether I shall come again."

"You'll say the same tomorrow when you leave," he said listlessly.

She went out of the room, banging the door behind her. She heard the bed creak slightly and then there was silence. He had obviously fallen off to sleep while all the 'right' things in his life were going about their 'right' business. While the avocado pear and aubergine lay in their ideal home of a wooden (made in Sweden) bowl, while the scatter of glossies glared on the table, while on the mantelpiece the 'right' people were at home to those who mattered. He slept, while the bamboo guarded and the kalim relaxed, and while the camembert no doubt ripened on its side in the kitchen.

Ruth stood outside the door, pursed her lips and sucked violently. She gathered the saliva into her mouth and landed one great contemptuous spit on the card that bore his name on the door. The name on the card was obliterated, and there was now nothing to show that Frank Woodfield or anybody else, dwelt behind the door. Neither after all, did it matter, she thought, by what name anonymity was called. She never went back. A woman can adulterate only once. Any subsequent fling is infidelity.

# 10

Their proposed holiday was only a month away, but neither attempted to plan for it. For Jack, the idea of not having anyone to miss or to come back to, seemed to make going away pointless. He was once again away on business and Ruth wasn't checking any more.

When Ruth awoke the first morning of Jack's absence the winter sun, absent for many weeks, suddenly turned up through the window like an intruder and reminded her of the holiday. She decided there and then to do something about it. She would buy a coat and some holiday clothes. She got up quickly and started to make the bed. Her side of the bed was scarcely disturbed, and she marvelled that despite the torment inside her she could sleep through a whole night with such apparent calm. She smoothed out the bottom sheet and, in one movement, covered the bed with sheet and blankets together. She looked at Jack's pillow. Newly-laundered and sleek from lack of use. She dimpled it for form's sake. Then she went to the window and drew the blinds to shut out the sun and in the light of her bedside lamp she dressed and made up her face. Coming out of the house the sun hit her again; she felt over-powdered and scented, her face a cocktail one, that called for the dusk as a backdrop. The main shopping centre was only a few minutes direct walk from her house but she decided to make a detour through the dark sunless alleys that led to the main street. On her way through one of these she passed the synagogue and stopped to read the day's text on the notice board outside. 'There is no darkness nor shadow of death where the workers of iniquity may hide themselves. . . . *Job*, Chapter 34, Verse 22.' She thought of Frank, and their dreary loveless affair. The idea that her sins were eternally visible frightened her. She read the notice once more, checking on its source. Job, thirty-four twenty-two, Job, three four double two, JOB 3422. Perhaps the number could offer her a hiding place. But from what? Sin was supposed to be pleasurable, yet she had had no pleasure from Frank. She had been someone else while with him and, even vicariously, she'd had no pleasure. She had dragged a second-hand mystique to his bed-sitter like a thief bringing loot to a fence. She recollected the mutual disgust, the nauseating performance of exchange, the drawn curtains that mercifully remained drawn even when it was all over, the lonely wordless departure into the festering clean bright air. If only she could have enjoyed it. It was no sin she'd committed, it was a punishment, a conscious self-infliction. Why then should she seek a hiding-place. Nevertheless, she ran into the porch of the synagogue as if to take cover. She reminded herself once again, as she always did when she passed this way, that really she and Jack should become members. Dying was such an expensive business if you weren't a member of a synagogue. A yearly subscription gave you the right to a seat and to certain benefits prescribed by the authorities. Among these was a piece of ground in the burial plots, with diggers and professional mourners thrown in. If they didn't join they would probably end up in a cemetery miles and miles out of town and the hearse would be as expensive as a taxi. Worse, they could end up by being cremated. Although in the long run this was cheaper, Ruth had an aversion to instant disposal. She had a vague belief in an after-life, in some form or another, and she wanted to give herself every chance. She started to go inside, resolved to affiliate, but she thought she had better consult Jack before making a decision.

She left the synagogue porch and walked out of the alley and found herself in the sun again. She felt her powder caking around her nose and she rubbed the small sweat spots on her nostril. She hurried quickly into the arcade of shops and was glad of the cool twilight inside. Outside the shop a picket line had formed, stiff as sentries, and as solemn. Each member carried a placard urging the public to boycott South African goods. The pickets were mainly teenagers with a sprinkling of middle class, middle-aged housewives to add tone. An old man with a sandwich board walked wearily up and down the line assuring all customers that, whether they observed the boycott or not, they could still buy goods at less than cost at the Railways Lost Property office. Ruth wasn't very politically conscious, but she read the papers and she remembered that this week had been put aside for an out and out boycott of South African goods. Ruth was in favour of the boycott and she felt guilty that she was not one of the line. She found difficulty in affiliating with anything. She walked past the line quickly, her forehead puckered in disapproval, for she was afraid to smile at the protesters in case they thought she was patronizing them. She entered the shop and made straight for the food self-service in the basement in which department the boycott would prove most effective. She would go down into the basement and positively boycott. She made straight for the fruit. A long double shelf was divided into heaped oranges, apples, bananas and pears. Each compartment was labelled with its origin, and the pile of South African oranges lurked at the end of the shelf like a gate-crasher. The oranges were packed in cartons of six and tied with a neat white ribbon as a last desperate bid for friendship with the English consumer. Ruth picked up a carton. "South African," she said to a floor-walker who was tidying up the shelves.

"That's right," he nodded with a smile, which quickly faded as she tossed them back on to the shelf as if she had picked up a pound of dandruff. The apples came humbly from England. Slowly and ostentatiously she took three packets from the shelf. She by-passed the grapefruit, the tell-tale badge of shame branded on their skins, and the tins of jams and fruit, all sneakingly labelled as 'foreign', which was a euphemism for the unmentionable, used by shop-keepers who already felt the pinch of the boycott.

A woman brushed past her and stretched out her hand for a carton of oranges. Ruth was about to stop her, when she guiltily remembered her own involuntary investment in the gold-mine. The reminder of the gift depressed her. She hurried to pay for her shopping. She wanted to get home quickly. She had nothing to do there, but there her indolence was contained. She would rush to her room, take off her clothes, and gratefully put on the old black skirt, jumper and slippers that was the uniform of her inertia. She would be herself again, and the depression would find its home.

A letter stuck out of the letter-box. She pulled it out as she turned her key in the door. The back of the envelope was stamped with the heading, 'BOKFONTEIN MYNBOU MAATS-KAPPY BEPERK'. She would change her clothes before she opened it. But when she was ready, she wanted to postpone it further. She made herself some coffee. To open the letter would have been an acknowledgement of the gift she had hardly accepted from Jack when he had handed it over. Once she had accepted the gift, she made herself payable. But Jack was not there to witness her acknowledgement. She opened the letter carefully, prepared to re-seal it for Jack's return.

"Dear Mrs Millar," it read. "We have been informed by our Head Office in Johannesburg that you have recently acquired some shares in the holdings of *Bokfontein Mynbou Maatskappy Beperk*. May we congratulate you and wish you, with every confidence, a great future in your investment.

As you already know, it has been the custom of our company over the years, to organize an annual international delegation of our more substantial shareholders to visit the mines and have talks with our administrators. This year, however, we are making a change in our normal procedure. Instead of a delegation, we are issuing over the year separate invitations to shareholders, not only to visit the mines, but as much of the Union as is possible. Moreover, we intend to spread our net, not only towards the smaller shareholders, but, for the first time, to women as well. As a bonus to your new status as a shareholder in *Bokfontein Mynbou Maatskappy Beperk*, may I extend an invitation to you and your husband to visit the Union, at our expense of course, and see for yourself how and where your investment is flourishing.

We would be happy to hear from you, and to send our representatives to call on you, should you accept our invitation."

Ruth did not read the letter over. But she replied to it immediately, referring to the letter only for the name and address of the sender. Without thought and in a scribble that was completely outside her, she acknowledged, accepted, stamped and posted, and when she came back from the letter-box, she read the letter again. Jack had given her more than he had intended and it irritated her that his conscience should be so generously served. Yet the prospect of the visit excited her. She suddenly recalled Aba Ben Saal, and the sad-dark he had promised her. Was it for this journey? She had already accepted the invitation, but she still had time to withdraw. Yet she knew how quickly she could reverse a decision, and how quickly reverse it again. She saw herself on the plane to South Africa, having decided never to be on it, strapped into her seat by her own lethargy, which was far less complicated than taking a stand.

The representatives arrived, three of them in a straight line, with a broad beam that stretched without interruption across their three faces.

"May we speak to Mrs Millar?" said one.

"I am Mrs Millar."

"We are from the Bokfontein Mynbou Maatskappy Beperk," the man continued. His face was suddenly solemn, but his two companions bravely sustained the beam, now intensified by the third man's share. "We have brought you good news," he proclaimed as if he had just dropped in from Ghent. "But of course," he added shyly, "you know already of our invitation."

"Yes, of course," Ruth said.

The captain of the team sat down, disappointed at her lack of reaction. "Such a wonderful opportunity," he mused. "Your husband will accompany you, of course?"

"Yes," Ruth said without conviction.

"Then you will be able to go together," he said cleverly. "A whole month in the Union," he said, "Oh how I wish I could go too. Christmas in the Cape," he reminisced. "I spent my childhood there." He paused, wistfully, while the others held the beam. Then quickly pulling himself together

– his childhood was either very short or very unhappy – he got down to business. "A South African aircraft will fly you there, of course, the best air-line in the world," he was fermenting with patriotism, "on Christmas day." He began to speak very quickly. "Everything will be taken care of. You will arrive in Johannesburg where a plane, South African, of course, will take you to Cape Town. There you will be met by our representative. We have a great tour planned for you. Cape Town, the Garden Route, Port Elizabeth, up to Durban and back via Johannesburg where you will stop off to visit the mines." He stopped suddenly, panting, as if he had run all the way. Then he began to smile, and the second man, who had been assigned the second paragraph, stepped forward with his piece.

"As you know," he said solemnly, "at the moment many people in this country have an attitude towards South Africa and her policies which is, to say the least, most unfortunate. I am sorry for those people because they do not understand." He paused for a moment to allow for some pity for the un-enlightened. Then his tone became belligerent. "But even though they do not understand," he shouted, "they see fit to meddle in affairs which are not their own. What do they do? They organize boycotts. Well," he allowed himself a smile, "I'm sure that *you* don't subscribe to that silly nonsense. Let them put their own house in order," he shouted, "and we will see to ours." He coughed modestly, laying the back of his hand to his poor forehead, so overburdened with knowledge, like a lay parson in a very bad film. "We have nothing to be ashamed of," he continued quietly, "as you, Mrs Millar, will see. You will see our natives, you will be infected by their happiness. You will see what we are doing for them, to raise them from their primitive way of life." He was dribbling with self-righteousness. "There are no problems in South Africa except those which people in England invent. We want you to see for yourself and to come back here and give the lie to all those stories that circulate about our country, to tell your friends that there is nothing but joy in the Union and brotherly feeling."

There was a rehearsed pause after this last little speech, while the captain stared at Ruth and timed the points going home. Then he nudged the third member of his team who stepped forward solemnly. "We have arranged with a newspaper, *The Daily Star*, to do a little feature on your trip. Our cameraman and a reporter will follow you around and every day we intend to publish a little story about what you've done and seen. With your permission, of course."

Ruth was still smiling and they assumed that permission had been granted. She could hardly contain herself at the thought of how wrong had been their choice of her, Ruth Millar, as ambassador of good will, and how bluntly she would refuse to co-operate with them. It would be a way too, of devaluing the gift Jack had given her. She was relieved when, after busying themselves with documents and further details of the trip, they left, well satisfied that their choice had been a fortunate one.

For a while after they had gone, Ruth considered how she would break the news to Jack. Should she stun him into the end of the story and then go into all the details that had led up to the invitation. Or should she start with preliminaries, tease him a little, withhold the result, lie a little to test what his reactions would be. She tried each way, using a mirror to discover what facial expressions would most excite him. But during the telling she lost interest in the whole business. A man had to love you very dearly before you could tease him without embarrassment. She even thought of dropping him a note – he would be up North for another two days –

and giving him the news cold. She no longer wanted to enjoy his reaction. She realized that she was a little afraid of it. Would he want to go to South Africa anyway? Though politically as inactive as she, she could guarantee his strong aversion to apartheid. And if he could be persuaded to go, Ruth thought, would he want to go with her? They would be forcibly thrown together into an isolation, six thousand miles from the site of his past affair, six thousand miles from the location of their home-made and self-generated tensions, six thousand miles from the grave of Jack's mother, thrown together into a vacuum of the present, at a crossroad that held neither their past nor their future, and made them both meaningless.

Jack was always glad to get home after his journeys, even though his home was often a weary battle-ground, but it was familiar and safe. He functioned there. He was in harness, no matter how uncomfortable it was. He felt excited as he put his key in the door. Even when he saw Ruth's shadow running through the hall to greet him his excitement did not wane. It was only when he saw her face to face that he felt his smile operating, consciously producing itself, pained with convention and the growing fear that perhaps Ruth noticed it. And she did. She noticed it every time he came home. She waited for it. She waited for the moment of change, and she knew when it came by looking at his eyes. Suddenly, like a spasm, the eyes which hitherto had joined the whole face in the smile withdrew, and the smile simpered solely on the mouth. Then she would kiss him, as if to obliterate the lie he was telling her.

"Did you have a good journey?" she asked.

"Not bad."

"Did you do well?"

"Not bad. How have you been?"

"Not bad. You hungry?"

"Not very."

Every time he came home from a journey their conversation was the same.

He followed her into the living-room. "Any news?" he asked.

"Not really."

"What's that mean?"

"Nothing."

Sometimes she wished that Miss Rallim had not left him. She sensed his frustration with the monotony of their lives together. She feared he held her responsible. She wanted his happiness and God knows, was it so terrible that she wanted it with her own.

She handed him a sherry. "Have a drink," she said. She poured a glass for herself.

"Here's to our holiday," she said. "Our second honeymoon."

"Oh yes?" Jack asked, not sure whether he wanted a second helping. "Don't tell me you've actually planned something."

"Oh yes," she said with supreme confidence. "I've planned it all. South Africa."

"What kind of joke is that supposed to be? I wouldn't go there if you paid me."

"I'll pay you," said Ruth. "Your fare, your expense, for a whole month."

Jack laughed nervously. He was half afraid that there was some truth in what she was saying. "On my own?" he asked.

"With me," Ruth said sadly. She half expected him to

say, "Who's me?" as Frank had asked her when she first came to him,

"Be serious, for heaven's sake," said Jack, finishing his drink. "What are you talking about?"

So Ruth told him the whole story, without any regard for her previous rehearsals, without any excitement or sense of climax, like a press reporter who transmits the basic adjectiveless facts about a crisis on a long-distance phone call.

"Well, that's fine," Jack said when she had finished. He was relieved mainly because the invitation had absolved him from the necessity of making a decision regarding their holiday together. "It'll be interesting to see the place anyhow," he said, without withdrawing his initial reluctance. "It's a joke, really, sending us of all people there."

"Mr and Mrs Millar," Ruth laughed, "ambassadors of good will to South Africa. It'll be our second honeymoon, Jack," she said gently, sitting on the arm of his chair. "Perhaps it'll mend us," she said sadly.

"Perhaps," he said kindly. He kissed her gently, recognizing in the prize a new avenue through which he could love her again. His mother had died and Carol had defected. They would travel six thousand miles into a new tension; a third party, depersonalized, necessitating no lies and no hurt, ever-present and accessible. The invitation was a godsend. It had to work. It would be his last attempt at a third party. He promised himself.

PART THREE

They had fastened their safety belts and eaten two barley suger sweets even before the plane had left the runway. Alongside them sat an old lady. Her eyes were tightly shut and she sucked violently at her sweet. In her hands she clutched her passport, as if, as long as she stuck to it, her identity was safe. She sat shuffling her feet close together, her shoulders rigid and her pale face drained with the pain of fear. She half opened her eyes and touched Jack on the shoulder. "Are we up yet?" she asked timidly.

"No," Jack said gently. "We haven't started yet. But don't worry. Any minute now."

"But I've nearly finished my sweet," she said frantically.

"Have some more." Jack had taken a handful. "And don't worry. Your first time up?"

The woman wasn't able to answer. All her thoughts were concentrated on the business of getting up into the air. She felt personally responsible for the operation. She tightened her safety belt and held another sweet at the ready. The plane began to move very slowly.

"I'm going to see my daughter in Johannesburg," the old lady muttered to herself. She tongued her sweet to the other side of her mouth. "I'm going to see my daughter in Johannesburg, I'm going to see my daughter in Johannesburg." Her voice was drained of any kind of conviction and after a few repetitions of the phrase she assumed a tone of protest. "But I *am* going to see my daughter in Johannesburg."

She kept this up until the plane stopped and turned at the end of the runway and thundered its engines in preparation for the take-off. The old lady clutched Jack's shoulder, petrified.

"My daughter's in Johannesburg," she shouted. She had already given up the idea of any further connection between herself and her daughter.

Jack stretched across the gangway to comfort her. He thought of the five stops on the way, the five landings and the five take-offs the poor woman would have to accommodate. He hoped she wasn't aware of them. "We're almost up," he said, "everything's fine. Just relax." He kept his hand on her trembling shoulder until they were up and climbing. "There," he said, "wake up. It's all over."

She opened her eyes and seemed surprised to find herself still sitting down. She smiled to herself and turned round to see if the others in the plane had been as fortunate as she. She was visibly glad to see that they had all survived.

"It was nothing, really," she apologized to Jack. "I'm just worried about my daughter in Johannesburg. She'll be coming back with me and she'll be terrified."

Ruth was looking out of the window. The plane was crossing over the field boundaries like a child playing hopscotch. After a while it came to the edge of the land and on the tip it seemed to hover as if to avoid stepping on the line. Then it crossed over to the sea, gradually shrugging off the uneven contours of the land, until beneath was only a vast still grey. The old lady looked down out of the plane. At first she couldn't make out what the grey was. All she was sure of was that it wasn't land. She didn't allow herself to think what it might be. Hurriedly she tightened her safety-

belt, and popped another sweet into her mouth, her own
personal safety precautions. Suddenly, with the sea as his
cue, an officer appeared at the bottom of the gangway
dressed in a yellow life-jacket, like a survivor figure. He was
grinning from ear to ear, not because he knew he looked
ridiculous, but because he was genuinely and mightily
pleased with himself. "Ladies and gentlemen," he said in
a strong Africaans accent, "may I have your attention."
There was a scattered silence on the plane; those sophisti-
cated travellers who'd seen the show before, continued with
their conversations. "Underneath your seats," the man went
on, "you will find a life-jacket. Like this one," he said,
pointing to his own. "Exactly like this one," he emphasized,
as if he had no intention of pulling a fast one on them. This
announcement in itself was enough for the old lady. Even
if it weren't the real thing, a rehearsal would only be tempt-
ing the gods. She let out a great wail, and called once again
on her daughter in Johannesburg. Jack stuck out his arm
once more to pacify her. But she was beyond comforting.
She wanted nothing to do with it, she screamed, she told
her daughter so, and she wished the silly yellow man, as she
called him, would go away. The man paused, while Jack
did his best to calm her. Suddenly she smiled at Jack, coyly.
"I'm old enough to be afraid," she whispered. "I'm over
seventy, and every day over seventy is a bonus from God. I
don't understand that yellow man. Even at his age I was
afraid."

"Take no notice of him," Jack smiled at her, squeezing
her arm.

The demonstrator had overheard. "Ladies and gentlemen," he said again, "this is very important. In a case of an
emergency, you will know how important it is. It is your
duty to survive," he said petulantly, as if it would be a re-

flection on the efficiency of the airline if they didn't play the game. "In a case of emergency," he relished the phrase, "you will dispossess yourself of all sharp objects, pens, pencils, glasses, shoes, dentures." The old lady indignantly clapped her hand over her mouth. "Then you will take your jacket," he went on, "which, as I said before, is underneath your seat. It is put on like this. Over the head and arms." He gesticulated wildly in the air. "When it is on, fitting snugly," he gave a sly smile, "you are ready to go. There are six emergency exits on the plane; you will see them marked on the side. On no account must you inflate your jacket before you leave the plane. Can you imagine," he grinned, "how difficult it would be if we were all blown up."

"I'm going to see my daughter in Johannesburg," the old lady whimpered.

"When you are out," the man went on, "you will pull this string, and the jacket will inflate." He pulled on the cord and the tubes obligingly swelled a little, slightly wrinkled like a tired balloon the morning after a party. "In the case of an emergency," he went on, as if the case were not emergent enough, "in case the jacket does not inflate, we have here a little valve. I put this valve in my mouth and I blow." He blew. "That's all," he said. "Simple, isn't it? And here," he said, touching a pocket in the jacket, "I have a little whistle." He blew again happily. "If I press this button," he said, touching the other side of the jacket mysteriously – his audience waited for the appearance of a white rabbit – "I have a flashing light." A pathetically small glimmer flickered from the torch. It was a down-beat end to the performance. "Now are there any questions?" he said disdainfully, as if it were at all possible that someone hadn't fully understood him.

"Excuse me, please. I have a question." A low dark voice came from the very back of the plane. The questioner who was acutely interested in his survival stood up. The demonstrator gasped. The man was black. It was true he wore a vicar's collar – he probably worshipped some witch god or other, the demonstrator thought – but he was irrefutably black. Jack turned round to look at the questioner. He had sat down again, alone on a three-seated bench, the very last bench on the plane. His position had been allocated. He sat there, clothed in his undeniable blackness, as madly as a Jew going to Germany in 1938.

"I'm sorry?" said the yellow man, straining his ear. "I didn't quite hear." He was bristling with rage. What right had this black man, vicar or no – he was making no allowances – what right did he have to understand the workings of a life-jacket? He had little enough right to live. Did he have to survive too?

The questioner stood up again. "Do we not observe some priority in our exit from the plane? Women first, and children. Perhaps you should make this clear?"

The yellow man almost exploded, angry at his own omission. The priority piece was first in his book of instructions. "That is something, I would have thought, would come naturally to all of us. Women and children first, of course, and then the gentlemen." He laid particular emphasis on the last word, ousting his questioner from the queue. In his mind he ran over his own personal priorities. First me, the man thought, then the women, the children, then the gentlemen. And the black man of God will come after me, after the children, after the women, after the gentlemen, after the baggage, after the freight, and, with luck, after the hereafter.

"Our holiday has begun," Ruth whispered to Jack. She

had a strange feeling of elation. It was like coming out of your own house to watch your neighbour's house on fire, with the excited sense of one's own security, mixed with the fear that it may not last. She took Jack's hand, and he hers. Like survivors they felt unbearably close to each other. She laid her hand on his shoulder. He stroked her hair and felt the sticky lacquer that covered it like a fossilized cobweb. She'd only recently started to use it. He shuddered at the feel of death in its texture. He took his hand away and clenched his fist to savour the stickiness. Then he fondled the unlacquered ends of her hair, and to the accompaniment of the old lady's repeated visits to her daughter in Johannesburg they landed bumpily in Zurich.

The flight was punctuated by transit cups of coffee. Between Ruth and Jack Millar there was no need for conversation. Nobody, least of all themselves, would notice that they did not communicate with each other. There were so many things to be busy about, and when they were done the actual business of sitting and waiting and being bored was a positive way of spending the time. It was not until the longest lap of the journey, between Athens and Nairobi, when they had read their books, had washed, had eaten, had looked about them, when it was too early to go to sleep, that it behoved Ruth and Jack Millar to say something, the one to the other.

"I'm tired," said Jack, getting in first with an excuse.

"Anybody would think you'd had a busy day."

"Well, I have. Busy doing nothing. Flying's such a bore."

Ruth sighed. It was her turn. Where did she go from there? And if she knew, was there any point in going there? "I'm beginning to get excited," she said.

"Why don't you try and sleep? Or you'll be too tired to enjoy yourself tomorrow. Here, put your seat back and lean on my shoulder. There," he said, gently fondling her head, "tomorrow you'll wake up in the sun."

She lay against him, breathing softly, taking care not to lay too heavily, knowing how easily his mood could be broken.

"Ruth," he said, "do me a favour."

She knew that his affection was already waning. "What is it?" she asked.

"For God's sake," he said, with sudden violence, "stop using that horrible lacquer on your hair." He had suddenly decided that the blame for all their unhappiness lay with Ruth's lacquer. "It's like putting your hand into a pot of jam."

"All right," said Ruth quietly. "I won't use it any more."

"You're a bit heavy," he said.

She took her head away and leaned back in her own chair. Jack took her hand by way of compensation, but she snatched it away. It didn't really matter which way the game was played. The words were always the same. Jack would hurt Ruth and Ruth would either accept the hurt or refuse it. Either way, the result was a temporary one, whether happy or miserable. All that mattered was that there would be a repeat performance, that the play, no matter how monotonous, would run for ever. And this perhaps was the only aspect of permanence in their relationship, and they each hung on to it, always ready to say their words, terrified of the moment when they would finally accept, each in their separate comas, the sheer misery of their having been landed together.

"The sun will make all the difference," Jack whispered. He was pinning his entire hopes on the removal of the lacquer and the appearance of the sun, and, highly confident, he quickly fell asleep with a light gentle snore. Ruth looked at him. Ever since their marriage he had been able to fall asleep as soon as he was tired, despite any unhappiness or anxiety. Ruth envied him for it. She turned her head from side to side, wanting desperately to sleep and to forget, wanting to believe in the sun's miraculous cure. The old lady alongside them slept fitfully, her fear still with her, reluctant to leave the pilot's seat, and take her hands off the controls. Some passengers were still reading, others staring ahead, frowning, full of those anxieties that accompany absences from home; the terrors of small, forgotten neglected things, the suspicion that one's house is not necessarily there if one is not looking at it, the panics that assume at night time such unnatural proportions. Ruth stared ahead of her too. She was not anxious whether her house was still there, whether the gas or iron was on, whether the pipes had burst or whether someone had stolen her silver. She cared less and less about possessions. She thought of Frank's bed-sitter and the desperate accumulation of material things, and she wondered what frantic thoughts he would entertain mid-air. She shuddered at the thought of her adultery. It was all Jack's fault and she trembled with a sudden hatred for him, wanting to hurt him, to deform him, to scratch like a cat on his face, to scar him forever for all he had and all he had not done to her. She turned to look at him. But in sleep he looked so innocent and so like a child she was tempted to tenderness. "Don't lie to me," she whispered, giving him a vicious dig in his chest. He looked about him helpless, and in his half awake state even more innocent than when he was asleep. "Sorry," she had to say, "my hand slipped." He smiled and closed his eyes again helplessly. She slid down in her chair. She put her arm round his tired body in an effort to catch his sleep. Jack slid his arm around her and brushed his lips on her forehead. She wondered how she could ever have given up hope for their marriage. She prayed silently for the continuance of his mood. His assured hand on her shoulder calmed her into sleep and when she awoke in the early morning the plane was already landing. The old lady was fast asleep, having left the controls and not even visiting her daughter in Johannesburg. Jack woke at the same time as Ruth, and the bright warm sun struck them as they became conscious, each of them simultaneously, of the undeniable presence of the other.

The old lady woke up as the plane taxied along the runway. She peered around her, half irritated and half relieved that the plane had managed to make the landing without her.

When they embarked again, Ruth noticed that the black man of God was no longer there. He must have been bound for Nairobi. He wasn't going on to South Africa, as if he had only wanted to go paddling.

The little old lady had unfastened her safety belt for the first time since they had left London, and was confiding to Jack that never again would she travel anywhere except by air.

The last lap of the journey to Johannesburg, punctuated by frequent meals, and a short stop at Salisbury, then meals again, seemed the shortest of them all, as if at Nairobi and their first glimpse of Africa, they had already begun to arrive.

# 12

At Johannesburg, the reporter whom Jack and Ruth had been promised waited at the barrier. "Mr and Mrs Millar?" he said, approaching them. A photographer stepped back and snapped them quickly as if there were a possibility that they would run away. The following day their picture appeared in the English *Daily Star* with the following article:

"Mrs Ruth Millar, a shareholder in the Bokfontein Mynbou Maatskappy Beperk, arrived in Johannesburg last night to start a month's holiday in South Africa, as the guest of the company. Her husband, Mr Jack Millar, was with her. They are a typical English couple, married two years and seeming to be on their second honeymoon. Radiantly happy, Mrs Millar told me how much they were looking forward to their trip. They left for Cape Town after a small reception at Johannesburg airport and there they will stay, visiting the beauty spots of the Cape, for two weeks. Every day we will bring you more of the adventures of this happy, lucky couple. Come with them to Chapman's Peak, Cape Point; swim with them on the beaches, and visit the picturesque locations. More tomorrow. Follow the Millars through South Africa."

The reception committee, six of them, were ranged against a table, laden with food and flowers. Their welcome was friendly and warm, and apart from a short speech from one of their number, informal. They talked of the flight, the marvels of modern communications, the weather, and the flight again. It wasn't until they were about to leave that Mr Badenhorst, their chairman, manoeuvred Ruth and Jack to one side.

"I hope you will enjoy your stay here," he said. "I don't know what your ideas about our country are like. An invitation is an invitation and it was issued without any consideration of your political opinions. But whatever they are, I'm sure that when you leave here in a month's time you will have the right thoughts and the right kind of understanding. We hope you will manage to see everything and without any pressures to come to your own conclusions. We have nothing to hide," he protested with the challenge of an amateur thief to an officer with a search warrant. "How is old England, by the way?" he changed the subject. "I love your country," he said defiantly, challenging them to do the same for his. "I was there during the war. They're a wonderful people. I stayed on a bit. I was in on the elections," he was obviously working his way deviously into asking a leading question. "And everyone seemed to take it so seriously. D'you vote yourselves?" he said, trying to appear off-hand.

"We vote Labour," Ruth saved him from further questioning. They had arrived. It would be pointless to send them back.

"Good, good," he said, and seizing the only advantage he could from the unfortunate situation, he said, "All the better. Then we really have to convince you, don't we?" He gave a sour smile. He heartily wished there had been a more efficient organization at the other end that had more thoroughly examined the credentials of its invitees. "I see we have a fight on our hands," he said, turning to the other members of the committee who had joined them. "We have one month, gentlemen," he announced solemnly, "to convert two Labour voters. Are we up to the challenge?" he asked heartily.

"Fine," said one. "There's no point in preaching to the converted."

"I think you misunderstand us," Ruth said. She didn't want to disappoint them so soon. "We're not prejudiced. We come with curiosity and an open mind. If we can see both sides of the problem, and if, as you say, you have nothing to hide, then we will go away with a better understanding."

Mr Badenhorst wondered whether she was playing him along. He'd never before met an open-minded Labour voter.

The plane for Cape Town was waiting, and an official had come to collect them. Mr Badenhorst walked between Jack and Ruth, and taking their arms he accompanied them through the airport lounge. On one side there were two doors each with a notice above them. Both doors led to cloakrooms; the one was labelled "Europeans Only", the other "Non Europeans". Ruth stopped.

"What do those signs mean?" she said incredulously, pointing at them.

It was a bad way to kick off, but Mr Badenhorst rallied. "One door is for us whites," he confided, "and the other is for the kaffirs."

There are some words, like kike, pimp, yid, coon, that carry within their offensive sound their own degenerate meaning, and it is impossible even by caressing such words on the tongue, to lessen the impact of degradation. Ruth had read about such notices; she had seen films that contained them and she had been remotely offended by their implications. But on seeing them, face to face, she was stunned by the sudden truth of it; she experienced a shock as basic as the shock of weaning, and as painful. She trembled and reached her hand over to Jack's, causing Mr Badenhorst to lag behind. She held on to Jack's arm, and he squeezed it and smiled at her.

Mr Badenhorst separated them again. They had reached the edge of the tarmac. The photographers were taking up their positions at the foot of the steps that led to the plane. "We will meet again on your return to Johannesburg," he said formally. He wasn't quite sure whether he wanted another meeting. He felt insulted by both of them. He had begun to feel quite indifferent towards their conversion. Something else, he couldn't quite define what, was troubling him. He hadn't liked them from the very start, even before the kaffir business. He found himself shaking Ruth's hand. "If, as you say, my dear Mrs Millar," he said coldly, "you have come with an open mind, then what you will see will speak for itself."

Ruth gave him a generous smile. "So I've already noticed," she said.

They waved from the plane and Mr Badenhorst stood watching the take-off. And as he stood there he suddenly realized what it was that had been troubling him all along. The Millars were Jews. That was it. So were lots of their shareholders, but it didn't mean that you had to go round handing them out invitations. It was asking for trouble. They might as well have sent along a couple of Communists. Automatically he waved his hand at the taxi-ing aircraft, praying in his heart that the plane, even though it was a South African one, would, with its cargo, crash ingloriously into the mountains behind the Cape.

Jack and Ruth sat close together in the half-empty plane. There was an unnoticeable silence between them. Jack put his arm round Ruth's shoulder, and she turned towards him. He kissed her gently, and when it was over, he recollected what he had done. And he felt an enormous gratitude that it had been so spontaneously possible. For Ruth, in that moment, all the former pain of her marriage was dissipated; the lonely evenings by the gas-fire, the infuriating quizzes, the horoscopes, her pathetic escapes from the consummate pain of rejection. She knew with sudden confidence that this moment was the norm, that everything else, the sense of outrage, fear and futility, was a diversion. After three hours, during which time hardly a word passed between them, the plane flew over Cape Town and gushed out over Table Bay to make a grand entry over the water into the city.

But their past together, Jack's infidelity, the lies he had sworn truly to her, had left in Ruth a residue of bitterness. During the course of Jack's affair, the hurt had settled and lay dormant. It was part of the overall sadness that enveloped her like a shell, a shell she had learned to accommodate and even to be at peace with. But when things were well between them the hurt awoke and nagged her. It prompted her to revenge, to destroy. She did not trust a time of peace between them, she feared it would end, and she would anticipate it by provoking a quarrel. It was a destructive urge in her, and illogical, yet she could not master it. Jack had so conditioned her to torment that peace frightened her. When they arrived at their hotel in Muizenburg on the shore of Cape Town she knew that, in spite of herself, she would provoke an unwarranted quarrel.

They arrived on Christmas Eve, and for their first three days they were free to laze on the beaches and to enjoy the less strenuous tours of sightseeing around Cape Town and Cape Point. A car had been placed at their disposal. The tour proper, their guide explained to them, would begin after the festive season. For some reason, it seemed, even in his brainwashed thoughts, that proselytizing over Christmas was rather indecent. He would wait until the mood of hatchet-burying and brotherly love had been digested, along with the Christmas fare, had occasioned the inevitable dyspepsia and the annual resolution never to indulge in it again. Brotherly love proved not only expensive but downright unhealthy, a folly that could be limited to only three or four days in the year. When the Holy Days were over and Christ wasn't looking, apostasy was free to put in a bid.

The guide deposited them at their hotel overlooking the beach. From the appearance of the foyer it was obviously a change-for-dinner hotel. Ruth looked at the guests loitering at the bar. Men and women, white as the day, she thought, and was perturbed that she had suddenly become so exclusively conscious of colour. She found their dinner jackets and long dresses, the outward show of gentility and civilization, as absurd as fancy dress at a funeral. The manager of the hotel welcomed them and she resented his friendliness. She knew she was being stupidly prejudiced, that one couldn't extend one's hatred of a principle to every human being who stirred within its orbit. Jack's reciprocal friendship to the man infuriated her, and as they were going to their room she grasped at an opening for a quarrel.

"I suppose you're changing for dinner," she said contemptuously when they were installed in their room. "Like the rest of them."

"What d'you mean? Changing for dinner has nothing to do with politics. There's plenty of things wrong with this country, but changing for dinner is not one of them."

"You can only afford such trappings if you've nothing on your conscience." She knew she was being unutterably stupid. It was a bait, and she was disgusted with herself for offering it.

"Well, I've got nothing on mine," Jack said.

"No?"

"No," he repeated. "You'll have to do better than that."

"Nothing on your conscience?" She tried not to say it, but the words squirmed on her tongue. "Not even Miss Rallim?"

It was a bull's eye. Between them, for the next half hour they used every weapon in the book. All but the very last, a weapon they each possessed, the power of leaving the one, the other, and it was the ultimate deterrent. But within these bounds the battle raged gloriously. It was at a point when Jack's forces were in the ascendant that someone knocked at the door. They collected themselves quickly, each waiting for the other to give the order for entry. They stared at each other while the knocking continued. Then simultaneously they both went to the door.

"Mr and Mrs Millar?" a man said. A group of photographers who had crowded behind him now swept past them into the room. They had set up their tripods on the balcony and around the room and were already photographing the luxury of the surroundings before the man at the door could state their purpose. "We're terribly sorry to disturb you," he said, "but we want a little something for the morning edition. You and your husband on the balcony perhaps, overlooking the magnificent view. Is it not probably the most beautiful in the world?" He had by now reached the balcony and Ruth and Jack followed him. Neither were in a sightseeing mood but it was difficult not to be impressed by the boundless stretch of white sand stamped with the shadows of the mountains like fallen sand castles.

"It's beautiful," they said, automatically. In her mind Ruth was going over the cards she had yet to play in her battle with Jack. She listed them in order of importance. She had been interrupted whilst on the defensive and so had a lot of ground to recover. She heartily wished the photographers would go. The man posed them together on the balcony and indeed they looked a miserable pair. "Shall we have a smile?" he said doubtfully, as if he were asking the impossible. They smiled.

"No, to each other," he suggested timidly stepping back to avoid an unexpected blow. They turned their heads to each other, holding the smile fixed on their faces with the assured conviction that neither of them could possibly mistake it for affection. "Once again," the man kept saying, while the team of photographers clicked away. "Perhaps one of you both sitting on the bed," he said daringly. Ruth and Jack took their smiles to the counterpane and gave them to each other. Ruth knew that if they didn't go of their own free will pretty soon she would throw them out. She wanted to cry out of herself the flotsam of bitterness that was corroding her. But it seemed after the bedspread snaps that the photographers had finished, but their leader wanted material for his copy. "I know you've only just arrived," he apologized, "but have you anything to say on your immediate impressions, Mrs Millar?"

"From what I've seen of the country," she said shortly. "I think it's beautiful. The scenery, that is. Just the scenery."

"Is that all?" the man was disappointed.

"There's more, but I doubt that you would want it." But nevertheless she decided to give it to him. "It seems a pity," she said, already aware of the stupidities she was about to utter, "that some of the people here, and they are a minority – a very small minority" – she laboured the point – "should be privileged to live in such an exquisite landscape."

The man doubted his hearing. He had obviously not been warned of the possible deviationist in Mrs Millar. "You must stay a little longer," he said weakly. "And you, Mr

Millar?" he hoped for something better from that quarter. Jack opened his mouth to speak, but Ruth, driven relentlessly by her own stupidity, stood up and decided to show them the door. "Get out," she said quietly, "and take your bunch of clicking monkeys with you. My husband and I wish to dress for dinner." The astonished man withdrew and in the manager's office with a trembling hand he wrote his copy.

Once she had included an outsider in her fury, the quarrel lost what little point it had. The battle never really got going again. They dressed silently and separately. When Ruth was ready she gave a final extra spray of lacquer to her hair and they went down to the dining room.

The restaurant was crowded. The manager who met them at the entrance explained that they would have to share a table for the evening, since the hotel was open that night to a conference of some kind. They would be given their own places in the morning. He led them over to a table near the window. A couple were already seated there. Both Ruth and Jack were relieved that they would not have to be alone together. The man of the pair stood up as Ruth took her seat. He smiled at them both. He was eager for communication. Perhaps, Ruth thought, he and his wife were inwardly as relieved as they were.

"I'm Ralph. Ralph Summers," the man volunteered, "and this is my wife, Priscilla."

Jack and Ruth identified themselves in return and the man smiled eagerly as if he recognized promise even in the names. By the end of the hors d'oeuvre they were a comfortable foursome.

"You're not South African, are you?" Ralph said.

"No, we're from London."

"On holiday here?"

"In a way," Ruth said, and she told them the whole story of the mining-company's invitation.

Ralph laughed. "Well I hope you'll say what they want you to say though, quite frankly, if you walk around with your eyes open, you're going to find it very difficult. How long are you staying in Cape Town?"

"Just a week."

"Like us," Ralph said. In his voice Ruth detected a sense of relief that others would share the responsibility of the holiday he had been obliged to take with his wife. Ralph was looking at her in a strange way as if to acknowledge a secret understanding. "D'you play tennis?" he said. The question was pointed directly at Ruth, as if he were suggesting singles. "There's a good court here."

"Yes, we could have a foursome," Ruth said. She was convinced by now what the man was getting at but she refused to acknowledge it. She understood Ralph's pressures. He had already been staying at the hotel for a week, he and Priscilla had had a long week of embarrassed silences behind them. She understood the enormous relief he felt that others had come to witness their coupling. That Ralph could say things that his wife had heard a hundred times before and know that for Jack and Ruth it was the first time. That Priscilla could indulge in her infuriating habit of patting her hair and Jack and Ruth might even find it charming. Ruth had experienced the same sense of relief at home when she and Jack were alone in the house and friends had unexpectedly dropped by. You didn't consciously change your behaviour but it seemed that the presence of a third party was a tightrope between Jack and herself. No matter how precarious or painful the crossing, it represented a possible means of communication. Here in this hotel even if she had to go via Ralph and Jack via Priscilla, they could come together. "Jack plays quite well," she said. She envisaged a foursome of mixed partners, the winners to play the losers. That way it looked more natural. And that, together with swimming, would at least take care of the day time.

"D'you play bridge?" Ralph asked. Ralph was a thorough planner.

"Sorry, no," Jack said.

Well, mustn't be greedy, Ralph thought. It didn't occur to him that the Millars would want some time to themselves. He wondered how they would pass their evenings. To him, the passing of the hours together was a mutual problem, mutually solved. "There's dancing here every evening," he said brightly.

Ruth looked from Priscilla to Jack and wondered how they would dance together.

"I'm afraid I don't dance very well," Jack said. He recognized in Ralph a picture of himself before he had met Carol. Ralph had probably been through a hundred Carols but Jack had exhausted that kind of third party. It was too unreliable. He had come to South Africa in the hope of finding a new formula, one that would involve no hurt, that would help disseminate the tensions between them. He looked at Ruth pleadingly.

Ralph was checking on his mental timetable. Mornings for swimming, afternoons for tennis and evenings for dancing. Pity Jack didn't play cards. It would have added variation. The week would pass quite quickly. Then he could get back home, give up his job, start to pack up and he and Priscilla could leave for England.

"D'you come here every year?" Ruth asked.

"Won't be here next summer," Ralph said, "Going to England."

"On holiday?"

"No. For good. We're going to settle there."

"D'you have any special reason for going?" Jack asked innocently. Ruth could see the foursome crumbling even before it had a chance to gel. "I suppose Ralph has personal reasons," she said, wishing to avoid an argument.

"Not entirely," Ralph took her up on it. "We're getting out for the obvious reasons. There's no future for a white man here. You can't live in a country like this without being involved. And involvement here means more than just taking part in a march or a sit-down. You've got to stick your neck right out, you risk your job, your family, even your life. You either involve yourself or you get out. There's no other way for a decent-minded white man."

Jack disliked Ralph. He had from the very beginning. He had sensed that Ruth had seen some function in this man and he wanted no part in it. Even now, when Ralph had given an opinion with which he could partially agree he disliked him none the less. It didn't seem right, somehow, that such a man could entertain the right kind of thoughts. He decided to argue with him. "I think you're being pessimistic about it," he said. "The problem will solve itself, naturally, given time. But if the whites up and leave, the justice, the strength and the guidance leave too. Then there'll be a massacre."

Ruth looked at him, horrified.

"I'll never understand that argument," Ralph said quietly. "Especially coming from your kind of people."

"My kind?" Jack knew what he meant, and immediately regretted having argued with him.

"Well, you're Jews, aren't you?"

138

Jack bristled. He hated the word. It was a sour hangover from his childhood in Germany. Just the sound of it, he hated. It was a sound that spurted from the spleen. It was a flat, monosyllabic accusation. Why couldn't the Jews be called by another name? Velvets, for instance, or nectarines. If someone had asked him what religion he was he would happily and even proudly have said, 'I am a nectarine'.

"After your history," Ralph went on, "you should recognize a red light by now."

"He's pulling your leg, Ralph," Ruth said, laughing weakly. "You don't know him." She leaned forward confidentially. "He's always pretending to believe in things just for the sake of arguing. Aren't you, darling?" she smiled at him.

"It's dull to agree with people all the time," he said. He hadn't given in out of weakness. It was just that he had little appetite for argument. Ruth's outburst in the bedroom saddened him. Bitterness did not become her; he knew it was all his doing. He tried to smile at her, but he didn't want to include anyone else in his message. He wished they could be alone.

"Let's not talk about politics," Ruth was saying. "Let's remember we're on holiday."

"Ruth is quite right," Priscilla said, patting the back of her head. It was the first time Priscilla had said anything. Ruth had the feeling she would agree with anybody.

"What are you going to do when you're in England?" Jack asked. Ruth smiled at him, grateful for his tardy contribution.

"Same line. Architecture. There's plenty going on there."

"You'll miss the sun," Ruth said.

"Well, climate's not everything," he laughed. "Is it, Pris?"

"No, you're quite right, dear."

Could Priscilla ever say anything else? Ruth wondered.
And why always *quite* right? Was quite right more right
than right, or less? And why did she always have to pat the
back of her hair when she said it? And if someone else
were to pat the back of her hair, would she still say it?
And did she ever say, "You're quite wrong?" She decided to ask her a question that would call for a specific
answer.

"How do you keep your hair so well-groomed?" Ruth
said. "You don't use lacquer, do you?"

Priscilla turned up her little nose. "No, I can't bear it,"
she shrilled. "Ralph likes a natural look, and he's quite
right, of course."

Ruth had a vision of Ralph and Priscilla leaning over the
boat-rail, mid-Atlantic, on their way to England, and Ralph
suddenly picking up Priscilla like a cat to be put out of
doors and dropping her unceremoniously into the sea. Before she went down for the last time Priscilla would pat
her little unlacquered head and say, gasping and spluttering, "You were quite right, Ralph."

The meal continued with intermittent conversation, which
became, with Jack's co-operation, increasingly friendly during the dessert. They teased each other cross-wise over the
table, Ralph poking fun at Ruth via Jack and Jack doing
likewise to Priscilla. The game was in its first joyous swing,
and familiarity exploded between them. The orchestra had
started up at the other end of the dining-room. It was a
waltz, undoubtedly. The violinist, who doubled as conduc-
tor for the small ensemble, was at pains to stress the first
of the triple beats by a lifting of one shoulder and a loud
tap with his foot. It was a waltz by sight. Ralph stood up.
He began his one, two, threes at the table, impatient to

reach the legitimate track, like a swimmer who warms up at the edge of the pool. He tapped Priscilla on her shoulder and his wife obediently stood up and patted her hair. Ruth waited for the remark that always accompanied that gesture. But Priscilla said nothing. It was clear that her hands and mouth were capable of working independently after all.

When they left the table, Jack and Ruth were undeniably alone together. "D'you want to dance?" Jack said.

"Do you?"

"If you want to."

"I don't mind."

They got up simultaneously. Neither wanted the other to suspect that they were guilty of *wanting* to do something. Jack slid his arm round Ruth's shoulders and guided her onto the floor. She moved close to him, stroking the back of his hand. She had a strange premonition of the return of the norm.

"You look lovely tonight," Jack told her.

Ruth patted the back of her hair. "You're quite right, Jack," she said.

He laughed. "Let's go for a drive along the beach," he said.

"What about those two?" Ruth nodded in the direction of Ralph and Priscilla. "Hadn't we better tell them?"

"We won't miss them, will we?" he said hopefully.

Ruth led him to the door. "Come quickly," she said, "so they don't see us. We'll explain in the morning."

# 14

As they drove away from the hotel the sound of music diminished and they picked it up again, on and off, like a hiccup, along the length of the beach front which was punctuated by hotels. It wasn't until they had driven beyond the limits of the official front that the utter silence began. The road was wide and bare. On one side lay an undisciplined scatter of bricks and building materials, as if a series of workmen had trickled to the place, had made a gesture and had left, driven away by the silence and isolation. On the other side lay the sea, as in a vast blue bed that had been undisturbed for a long time. It breathed fitfully in small white ripples. On the sands a few small dunes sprouted with grass, lazy sentinels, guarding a sleeping sea, that no one in any case wanted to disturb. The silence and desolation stretched along the coast for many miles of straight white road. It was a no-man's land for carefree strident passage, for a sense of momentary power and freedom, with the fear and excitement of what lay on the other side of the border. At the end of the straight the road began to turn, and so, from the gathering momentum of the sea, did the tide. At the beginning of the new road Jack let the car run to a stop, astonished by the sudden change in landscape and the abrupt anger of the sea. It was then that both of them recollected the silence that had accompanied their own silence for the last few miles. And both with relief, because it had been a silence that neither had noticed at the time. On one side of the road the scattered bricks of the no-man's land had gelled into mountains, stencilling the sky with black irregular peaks, like an unstable sales chart. And on the other side the sea had got out of bed, furious, dashing its white anger against the lumps of black rock that impeded its passage to its mute sandy lover on the shore. Ruth and Jack left their car and walked down towards the beach. Ruth took off her shoes and watched her toes sift the sand as they walked. Small grains settled round the cuticles of the nails, freckling the red varnish. A few yards ahead of them they could see two notice boards, one alongside the other. They reached the first. The notice was printed in large bold shameless letters. "THIS BEACH IS FOR NON-EUROPEANS." Ruth was amused by the finesse of the terminology that was meant to compensate for the poison of the principle. "Non-Europeans," Jack muttered. "Such a gentle, inoffensive word; like this beach is only for nectarines. Why can't they say what they bloody well mean?" he shouted. "Only lousy kaffirs can come here, only lousy yids, chinks, kikes, queers, lepers." He was beside himself with fury. He listened to the echo of what he had just said. He'd said yids, hadn't he, he'd lumped them all together. He was aware that he had achieved a new perspective. "Yids and kaffirs," he muttered to himself. He remembered the night in the house with Ruth, when he had screamed "why" to the dead white walls. It was the same here. He picked up a stone, and with impotent rage hurled it at the notice and the sound was swallowed up by the raging sea. Ruth had moved over to the other board and she motioned Jack to join her. "BATHING IS DANGEROUS HERE," it said. Jack clenched his fists. He knew that if a white man had suddenly appeared he would, without any questioning as to his opinion, have killed him on the spot. He leaned against the notice, obliterating its obscenities. "Why, why," he muttered.

Ruth was staring out at the sea. The undertow was dragging back the reluctant pebbles on the sand. She fixed her eyes on one large stone and followed its progress; a large wave caught it on the shore and scooped it up like a crane, embraced it in its foam, teased it a little in the surge of its swell and finally mastered it in a white roaring spasm.

Jack came to her side. He heard the noisy tantrums of the sea and in its echo heard his own indignation. He put an arm round Ruth's waist. "We must stay together," he said. "Whatever happens, whatever happens between us, I know that it's right that we should stay together."

Ruth started to walk towards the water. She had more than understood him and she feared any further words between them that would have degenerated into meaningless vocabulary. Jack followed her silently. They climbed the intermittent dunes until they came to a stretch of white sand where the sea, resting a while, gently lapped its shores. In front of them, on the edge of the water, was a small black rock, fixed firmly in the sand. Occasionally the tide would reach it, lick it in homage, and turn back. Jack lay down and pulled Ruth to his side. He watched the sea and regretted its momentary calm which in no way corresponded to the feelings that raged within him. He leaned over Ruth, and knew, for some reason or another, that she must be identified with the woman he married. Not Carol, not Mr Rallim, nor any of the witches who punished him in his dreams, not even his mother – yes, he had to admit that, too – this was Ruth with the black long hair, the brown eyes, the pointed chin, the round full breasts, the mould of belly smooth as a sand-dune, the thighs, yielding like the pebbles on the shore to the lustful thrust of the sea. He turned his back on the water, and like an oncoming wave sought to reach his own private shore. He heard the water behind him turning over in its waves, gathering with each thrust an added momentum, breathing in deeply, and almost, almost breaking, but pulling back to gather more power. And then, its lungs full, and unable to hold its breath any longer, it broke in one final white torrent onto the waiting pebbles. For a moment, Jack listened to the singing echo of the sands. "Ruth," he said.

She took his throbbing hand. They lay beside each other, the "why" moment momentarily drained out of his body, leaving no vacuum.

When Ruth looked up she noticed that the black rock in front of them had moved. It was still wet and shone with an ebony lustre although the ebbing tide had not touched it for a long time. The caked sand below it had cracked, unable to bear the weight. Jack was staring at it too. Since they had left the hotel everything had become so unreal, so inexplicable, that he was not surprised when the black rock, deserted by its foundations, slowly and clumsily keeled over. He stood up and, taking Ruth's hand, led her towards the rock. The moon was almost directly above them and it beamed on the black mound like a spotlight.

It was a seal, a bull-seal, and its body bore the scars of battle, jagged irregular rents, like Caesar's mantle. And he, too, had probably been a Caesar who with ruthless tenderness had dictated a distant colony. But age had overtaken him, and, too old for the cows, his younger and erstwhile friends had fought him out. He had become as redundant as ripeness. Yet from the wounds on him, he had put up a great fight. The white horses of the sea had borne him to the shore, roaring about him the injustice of his exile. And he had kept his proud dying till out of earshot of the colony, when, cradled by the waves. he had roared his last offended breath. A half hearted attempt had been made to bury him, but the sea had licked away the sandy vault. Jack bent down to touch him.

He was bigger than his spider, and beyond all function. There was nothing enviable about the black impotent exposure on the sand. Yet Jack felt the same affinity with it as he had with the industrious spider whose work he had so jealously destroyed. He felt the why creeping into his throat. He had thought, lying on the sands with Ruth a few moments ago, that he had solved everything, that joy was reachable, and now this crippled palsied seal had splintered the illusion. All his life he had struggled with the fear of impotence. He remembered Helmut Kahn and his phylacteries. Helmuth hadn't lived long enough to test his manhood, but at least he'd been given the key. He thought of his mother without bitterness. He carressed the sleek oily surface of the seal's body outlining with his fingertips the wrinkled contours of the polished skin, swollen with the sad senility from which the seal had died. Jack drew his hand away quickly. He stood up and realized that Ruth was beside him. "Let's go," he said quickly.

The wet border of sand had widened and the beginnings of the sea wailed their distant echo, as if the tide had gone out and never intended to return. The moon had slipped down the sky and brought the white sand more sharply into focus. They climbed the small dunes that led to their road. On the down slope of a sand dune they saw the bent black figure of a man watching them. It had been some time since either of them had seen a living being, and at first they thought the figure was a stray rock that had sprouted, unsired, from the sand. As they approached it the figure swayed, as if in prayer, and slowly moved towards them. Ruth tightened her hold on Jack's arm, and he on hers, for neither of them in the climate of unreality that had recently enveloped them both, had any confidence in anything that appeared to be alive. The man walked slowly towards them, and then, within a few yards of them he stopped and they felt obliged to stop too. He was black, and the moon zoned his face into single and seperate features. His skin was wrinkled, or rather, pleated, for the folds fell neatly and apart. On his head he wore a peaked Basuto hat, and his fuzzed grey hair frayed like a trimming below the brim. A torn red shirt lay on his bony chest and baggy trousers that could have accommodated three of him stood around his legs. His feet were sore and bare. Ruth looked at them intently. She was counting his toes. Seven on one foot and eight on the other. She counted them again, thinking that the moonlight had deceived her, but the figures were the same. The man was watching her as she counted.

"I've got enough toes, missus," he said, "for three feet." He held out a skinny hand. "I'll give you a foot's worth for a tickey," he said. Ruth and Jack moved sideways and ran, their knees pained with fear, over the sands to the road. The man looked after them, then at his unprofitable toes; he grabbed a clump of grass out of the sand, and with it he beat his toes sore.

When they returned to the hotel, Ralph and Priscilla were sitting on the terrace waiting for them, bewildered as two bridge players whose partners had unaccountably disappeared. Jack drove round to the back entrance and they went straight to their room.

Lying in bed, Jack tried to unravel the discoveries – and he knew they were no less – that had interrupted the evening. On seeing the seal he had been squarely faced with the fact that you could die from impotence. That, he decided, was the first revelation. Secondly, he remembered that he had, in one swift thought, thrown the Jew and Negro together on the notice board and found that they had mixed without curdling. The discoveries persisted in remaining separate to his mind, yet he knew that somehow they were closely related to each other. He sensed that his own problems were linked to that relationship and that if he could discover the nature of it he would at last feel free. And having achieved freedom within himself he could love Ruth without the need of detours, the two of them, alone and together, face to face.

# 15

When they awoke on Christmas morning it was unbearably
hot. The sun crowded in at the windows, spraying the room
in dust-laden beams of heat. Even the sound of the Birthday
bells from the church nearby were flattened by the broiling
sun. Ruth wilted out of bed. She walked out on to the
balcony and watched the Christmas streets below. Bare
armed strollers, shops closed with sun-blinds and small
brown boys, who should be carolling winter-booted, diving
into the sea to shelter from the sweltering heat. She found
it hard to accept the idea that Christ was born under a
blinding sun. It was cold, bitterly cold, and snow lay on
the ground. It was the moon that shone brightly, as it had
last night on the dead black seal. And in the morning the
frost had come, not the oily sun surfaces that glimmered
from the streets below. He was born cold and holy. How
could she possibly acknowledge His birth in these sun-
drenched streets racked by the flattened bells.

She turned to look at Jack on the bed. She wanted to go
to him and wake him up with love. But she was afraid. She
knew that something had happened last night; she knew
that in a way he had been happy, and that she had been part
of it. She felt suddenly grateful to him, and almost as suddenly, resented her gratitude. She wished she could feel
herself free with him, free to love him, to tease him, to

get angry with him, without fear of his reactions. But she was afraid. She had to admit it. She was afraid of him. She wanted him to be happy. Of this she was sure. But she felt she was an impediment and she thought he thought it too, and it was that that made her afraid. And once again she became resentful that he should regard her as an obstacle. Sometimes she wanted to hurt him and almost at the same time to give him joy. She shuttled daily between the two extremes. And sometimes in her worst moments she hovered between, shivering with her love and her hate, like a giant string that plucked, vibrates for ever.

Jack was getting up. She avoided his look, because she couldn't bear him not to smile at her. Yet he would be angry with her if she didn't at least say good morning or throw off some comment that showed that she was aware of his presence in the room. She went over to the bed and with mock formality said good morning. He looked at her, startled to see her, as if he had been under the impression that he had slept alone. "Good morning," he said. They were like two clerks meeting behind a bank counter.

He went into the shower, locked the door and took off his clothes. He saw himself naked in the mirror, and studying himself, he faced the fact that it was Christmas morning, in a black land, and that he was a Jew. And last night he had seen the dead seal. He smiled. He had thought of each fact associatively. He was right. There was a connection between them. If he could only define the shape of the pieces, he was confident he could fit them together. "Are we going to Cape Point, today?" he shouted through the door.

"Yes," Ruth answered. He felt her waiting. "Shall we take Ralph and Priscilla along?" she added.

Jack had forgotten about them. He wanted to go on

trying without their help. But perhaps Ruth liked them. And in any case he had a jig-saw to put together. "If you like," he said.

"What about you?" Ruth didn't want to take the responsibility.

"I don't mind," he said. He heard an accusing silence outside. "All right," he added, "let's take them along."

They breakfasted with Ralph and Priscilla. No reference was made to their sudden disappearance the previous evening, as if Ralph and Priscilla were prepared to put up with any minor rejections on the road to ultimate surrender. They were confident, Ralph knew, or thought he knew, that the Millar's need was as great as their own. It was taking the Millars a little longer to recognize it perhaps and he would allow them a show of struggle before they would finally succumb. Meanwhile, he and Priscilla would be waiting on the terrace.

"Next year, you'll be seeing a white Christmas," Ruth said.

"You're quite right," said Priscilla. She was at her old head again.

Ruth wondered whether she was up to taking Priscilla's patting and quite righting for a whole day. She would wait for Jack to issue the invitation.

"Don't take much notice of Christmas myself," Ralph said. "It's nice for the children, of course," he went on, "but then we don't have any, do we, Priscilla?" He turned to his wife. She opened her mouth and raised her hand to give the usual response, then realized that he was not asking her opinion. He wanted only confirmation. "No," she said flatly, but she had to pat her hair all the same.

"What about coming to Cape Point with us today?" Jack said. Ralph smiled eagerly. "It's our first down-payment

on the prize. Something nice and uncontroversial to start
off with. We'll have to take the guide with us of course, but
I think he'll take his own car if you're coming."

"But he'll want to point out the places of interest on
the way. Simonstown, for instance." Priscilla had never
mouthed so much. The prospect of a drive to Cape Point
had somehow excited her, and brought her, such as it was,
into her own. "D'you know," she confided to Ruth, patting
her stupid little head, "I was born in South Africa and
I've never been to Cape Point."

"Then it's a date," Jack said. He was in a good mood,
and Ruth acknowledged it gratefully.

The guide however insisted that they all come in his car
which was a bigger one, and more comfortable. He didn't
take too kindly to tagging along the extra two. In fact he
didn't take kindly to the whole excursion. He hated the
Millars. Especially her. She had thrown him out of her
room in front of a bunch of cheap photographers and he
would never forgive her. He had talked himself into thinking that he wasn't necessary on this trip anyway. They
could find their own way to Cape Point quite easily; you
just had to go on and on. They wouldn't be guided around
Simonstown, it's true, but then it was almost theirs and
they would resent it anyhow. Nothing could go wrong with
a Cape Point excursion; the worst that could happen was
that you could fall off the edge of the world, or be ravaged
by the Cape Point monkeys. The way the guide felt about
Mr and Mrs Millar he didn't mind which exit they chose
as long as they never came back. The Bokfontein Mynbou
deserved a death or two on their hands for their thorough
incompetence. No. They could definitely go on their own.
Then he caught sight of the camera that hung round his
neck and he remembered that the paper wanted photo-

graphs. "Mr and Mrs Millar at Cape Point" or, perhaps, he thought wistfully, "Their guide pushing them over."

"My car's the black sedan," he shouted. "I'll see you round the front."

They all tried to pile in at the back. It seemed that no-one wanted to sit by the guide. Ruth suddenly felt sorry for him, and repented that she had treated him so badly. She slipped into the front seat beside him. She was happy that Jack was happy and she wanted everybody to be happy too.

"I'm sorry about last night," she said to the guide. "I behaved terribly towards you. I'm really really sorry. We'd been travelling you see for what seemed like weeks," she confided, "and we were so terribly tired." Involuntarily she shared the blame with Jack. "We were just irritable and hungry, I suppose. Forgiven?" She smiled up at him.

The man melted completely. He had more than forgiven her. He was prepared to marry her on the spot. The whole car-load was now throbbing with good humour and the guide had second and kinder thoughts about the Bok-fontein Mynbou. They passed St James' beach, quietly built into the coastline like a sand-lined pocket and along to Fishhoek. Here, although it was Christmas day, the Cape coloureds were at work, dragging in their nets and their livelihood. The guide – he had asked them to call him Jan; "That's my real name," he confided, as if he had at one time considered giving them a false one – stopped the car and guided them on to the sands to watch the fishing.

At the far end of the beach a line of fishermen stretched from the water's edge over the sands to the sea wall. A long rope passed through their hands, secured to the waist of the last man, its other end affixed to the net somewhere out at sea. They walked slowly towards the centre of the beach easing the rope out of the water as they moved. There was no sense of purpose on their faces and no anticipation. After years of sieving the sea they knew the miserable catch that would fall to them. There were twelve men in the line and each with a stake in what the sea would yield. But this was only half of them. Coming towards them from the other end of the beach was a similar line of unexpectant faces, easing in the rope with a practised tempo in their hands. Between them, out in the sea, was a great semi-circle of bobbing corks, outlining the limits of their catch. As the two lines converged, the spectators who stood between them, children of the beach, fishermen's wives, and Jan and his party, backed towards the sea wall, where they waited for the meeting of the lines. Neither side was in a hurry. It wasn't a show for tourists; it was a means of livelihood, and there was nothing abnormal or quaint about it. And it took time. The audience waited almost an hour before the beginnings of a net were visible. Finally the lines came together. Fisherman faced fisherman without acknowledgement. In silence the pulling began and gradually the net was dragged on to the shore. A few of the men started to laugh when the catch was visible, and they teased out of the net the wriggling dog-fish that had misleadingly weighted the catch, and threw them back into the sea. It had taken the labour of twenty-four men, an enormous net with its wear and tear, about an hour and a half in time, and the end result was no more than about seven pound of mackerel. The men wearily bundled the fish into wooden boxes, and out of nowhere came the town's housewives to bargain for the catch.

They turned to go back to the car. A net was hung out to dry on the sea-wall, and as they passed behind it they saw a young girl, probably one of the fishermen's daughters, spreading the surplus out on the sand. Her bronzed thigh darted out of the slit in her dress as she bent down, and Jan surreptitiously lagged behind. Pretending to examine the nets, he began to enjoy her. Ruth looked at him and saw him ogle the girl's thigh and bite into her flesh. His face was red with wanting. He caught Ruth looking at him, bent down to finger the net, and walked quickly on. As he came alongside her, Ruth muttered, "It's not much of a living, is it?"

"They don't know any better," he said angrily.

They piled into the car and drove towards Simonstown. Jan was sulking and from the silence in the back of the car the happy mood of the passengers had obviously evaporated.

"Our last Christmas in South Africa," Ralph untimely announced from the back of the car. He couldn't bear the silence any longer. Jan squirmed in his seat, clenched his teeth and said nothing. The car swerved round a bend and they drove on for another five minutes in silence.

"You're quite right, dear," Priscilla was having a delayed reaction. Ruth looked in the front mirror and caught Priscilla's hand descending. As they drove along the beginnings of a village sprouting through the green borders of the road. Ahead of them lay a harbour and sundry ships at anchor. On one of these ships the crew was visible, standing in formation and singing. Through the noise of the car engine they could hear the strains of a carol and Ruth wanted Jan to stop so that they could listen. But Jan accelerated and tore through the town. When they reached the countryside again, the carol was still audible. "That was Simonstown," Jan said spitefully. He turned to Ruth and smiled. He'd had his own back on her for catching him wanting the fishergirl. He was ready to be happy now. "We'll stop at Simonstown on the way back," he promised. "There's a bit more life there in the evenings."

At the back of the car Jack had started on his jigsaw, but with a sudden pang of homesickness, occasioned by the carol-singing of the English sailors, which interrupted his calculations. He wondered why something as alien as a Christmas carol sung by Englishmen should stir within him certain feelings of patriotism. Was this another piece he had to fit into his puzzle? In any case, he realized, any jigsaw worth its name had to have at least a hundred pieces before it could add up to a decent picture. He put the patriotic piece on the side for a moment, and returned to the shape of the seal, with which he was more, though disturbingly familiar.

For the next few miles there were no signs of habitation, though the landscape, verging on the edge of the earth, gave a final spurt of fertility. In silence they reached the iron gates of the Cape Point Reservation and after a few formalities they drove through. Jan had decided that he would deliver them on the Point, take his pictures, rush back to the café down the road, take some refreshment, perhaps a little sleep and wait for them there. He became suddenly talkative with the prospect of his being soon on his own. "I used to come down here as a boy," he said as they drove through the parkland. "The zebras were bigger then and the springbok. Every time I came down here I used to see them, but you have to be lucky to catch sight of them. Grown-ups aren't so lucky, I don't think."

"There's some," Ruth shouted, pointing over the heath. Jan stopped the car and they looked out. A pair of unconcerned zebra nuzzled each other in the heather, the sun striping the green with their shadows. Beyond them like a shooting star a springbok broke out of the grass and vanished.

"We're lucky today," Ruth said.

"They were bigger when I was a boy," Jan started the car again.

"D'you like animals?" Ruth asked. In spite of herself she was beginning to like the man.

He laughed as if the question had been a stupid one. "I grew up with them," he said. "My father's a farmer. He's moved up to the Transvaal now. But here in Cape Town, when I was a boy, I grew up with them. There's nothing else in life, heh?" he said suddenly. "D'you know," he confided, "once when I was ill in bed and I couldn't come up here and I couldn't play with my pets, I used to stare out of the window. Day after day," he mused almost to himself, "I used to stare at it. Why even that mountain gave me pleasure."

"What? Lion's Head?" Ralph joined in the conversation. "You've seen it, Ruth, haven't you?"

"Yes," said Ruth. "We saw it yesterday on our way to the hotel. It doesn't look like a lion's head to me."

"Have you ever seen a lion?" Jan asked.

"Lots of times."

"Then lions are wrong," Jan concluded.

At this point Ruth would not have minded if Priscilla had given her usual approval. For the first time, it would have been appropriate. She approved of Jan more and more and even Jack momentarily took his mind of his jigsaw to pay the man his silent respects.

They reached the end of the road and parked the car along with many others on a flat circular piece of ground overlooking the sea. The point itself could not be approached by car. You had to walk up a steep hill to reach it. On the parking space the monkeys abounded, hopping from car to car. As Ralph got out of the car a monkey hopped by and swiped his glasses from off his nose, disappearing with them into the undergrowth. Everyone found this incident amusing, except for Ralph who stampeded up and down, demanding of the empty air the return of his property. Through the bushes the monkey could be seen trying on the glasses and, finding that with them, he viewed matters in quite a different light, he decided to explore further into the bush to re-discover his familiar habitat. No amount of coaxing from the spectators could bring him out. There were no keepers in sight, and Ralph was cursing the authorities of the Cape Point Reservation for their negligence, threatening to sue, and enduring Priscilla's continuous approval. All this time Jan had stood some way off, taking his photographs at leisure and seemingly indifferent to the recovery of Ralph's property. When Ralph became practically hysterical at his loss, Jan approached the undergrowth. Everyone made way for him, scenting his authority. He got down on his knees and let out a strange call. It was a soft vibrant sound and low pitched, but its echo through the bush was thunderous. Almost immediately the monkey was visible, searching for the source of the cry. Straining his ears, he took off his glasses in order to hear better. Jan called again. The monkey spotted him and leapt towards him. Jan waited. He was in no hurry. The spectacles were easily within his grasp, but he made no move to take them. He wasn't going to humiliate the monkey in front of all those people. He held out his hand, and the monkey clasped it in his own. Then, together, they crawled into the bush.

After a short while the bushes fidgeted and Jan, slightly dishevelled, crawled out from underneath. In his hand he held the spectacles, but one of the arms had broken off. Ralph came towards him. "I'm sorry," Jan muttered. "That was the best I could do."

"Why did you have to put up a fight for them?" Ralph

said disdainfully, and taking his glasses he started out towards the point. Priscilla panted after him, and Jack and Ruth, with Jan rattled and flustered between, followed them.

Jack was confused. Every moment he seemed to collect another new piece. He hoped that they belonged to other people's jigsaws. Ralph's for instance, or even Jan's, though he shuddered at the contortions of Jan's pieces. Since he had seen the seal and suspected its symbol his mind had become a mirror, reflecting and throwing back images and thoughts with astonishing clarity. Incidents which hitherto had no meaning or connection suddenly became significant and involved. He had so much thinking to do. He longed to imprison himself up in a room, to shut off his mind to new experiences until he had sorted out the material that he had already acquired. He looked across Jan at Ruth and was surprised to feel how remotely he thought of her. Her too he wanted to shut out until he had achieved some order. He had, somehow or other to make arrangements for his own incarceration. It was vital to him.

The trek up the hill was slow and in the noon-day heat, painful. Ralph and Priscilla were disappearing round the side of the hill, and Ruth saw her pat her head, and she wondered to what latest profundity of Ralph's she had given her sanction. At the top of the hill they rested. Jan sat down on the side of the road, mopping the sweat off his face. He too needed to be alone, and Jack motioned Ruth to leave him for a while. They turned to go up the steps to the bridgehead. It was the first time since early morning that they had been alone together.

"I can't bear those two," Ruth said.

"They're not too bad," Jack was disappointed that she had lost interest so soon. At the moment he didn't want her exclusively. He might even have been glad, at least in theory for Ralph to take her off his hands. "If he'd broken my glasses, I wouldn't have taken it too well either. He's pretty blind without them."

"You're more tolerant than I am," she said, taking his arm. They reached the bridgehead together, and found Ralph and Priscilla already there, leaning over the rail.

"You're a long way from home," Ralph said. One would think it would be possible to lean over one end of the world, a position one doesn't assume every day, and keep one's mouth shut. But Ralph had a talent for rendering everything pedestrian. He could have taken the magic out of the sunrise. The remark was ignored. Even Priscilla let it rest. Perhaps she understood that it was Ralph's way of stating that he was once again available for conversation.

The Atlantic drifted on one side of the point and the Indian Ocean on the other, seagulls flew over from one sea to the other without wonder. As far as the eye could see there was nothing, not even a meeting of the skies and the water.

Jan was suddenly behind them. "It's a beautiful country, heh?" he said sadly as if he didn't want to acknowledge that it had a boundary. Ruth smiled at him. "Would you like some pictures here?" she asked. Jan went to work quickly without disturbing them, then he left them to wait in the car.

When the foursome reassembled after the photographing, Ruth found herself with Ralph and Priscilla with Jack, and nobody knew who had engineered the switch over. Ralph took Ruth's arm and led her down the steps. "I never got round to dancing with you last night," he said.

"We felt like some fresh air, so we went for a drive." Ruth wondered what Jack was saying to Priscilla. She knew without looking what Priscilla was undoubtedly saying to Jack.

"Shall we manage to get together tonight?" he asked. "On the dance floor, of course," he added, though his tone of voice indicated that he was not too fussy about the location.

"If you like," Ruth said vaguely. "If it's not too crowded in there."

"I've got a lovely balcony to our room. We could dance there." Ralph only had a week left of his holiday. He couldn't afford the refinements of preliminaries.

"We'll see." Ruth didn't want to hurt him. But she began to dislike him intensely. She turned to look at Jack, and discovered his arm in Priscilla's. And though Ralph was holding her in the same way she felt suddenly resentful. Jack was silent and Priscilla was talking volubly. Occasionally Jack nodded his head, or tried to get a word in. Then Jack laughed happily and agreed with her again. Ruth stood still and Ralph was forced to wait too. As the other couple came towards them, Priscilla was chattering more and more, and Jack kept on nodding his head in agreement. Any moment Ruth expected him to start patting the back of his hair. They came alongside, and they sat, the four of them together, half way down the slope. In Ralph's presence Priscilla was suddenly silent. Ruth noticed a glow on her face that she hadn't seen before. She caught her fingers stroking Jack's hand as she took her arm out of his. They were obviously moves ahead. At this signal Ralph turned to Priscilla. "What about the party tomorrow night?" he asked.

"That's a good idea," said Priscilla. "D'you think," she hesitated, "d'you think they'd fit in. I mean, d'you think they'd play the game?"

"What game?" Ruth was startled.

"Just party games," Ralph said quickly. "Nothing special. Just the sort of things you do at most parties."

"I think they'd like it," Priscilla said.

"What party are you talking about?" Jack said impatiently. He didn't like being discussed as if he wasn't there.

"We've got some friends here," Ralph said casually. "They give wonderful parties. Not terribly interesting people, but their parties are pretty well-known in Cape Town."

"Why? What's so special about them?"

Ralph hesitated. "They're fancy dress for one thing."

"There's nothing special about that," Jack said.

"No, they're not so special," Priscilla cut in. "They're just good parties. But we'd have to let her know whether you're coming or not, wouldn't we, Ralph? She tends to be pretty organized."

Ralph smiled. Priscilla had expressed it perfectly. "Yes, we'll have to let her know tonight. Will you come?" he turned to both of them. "Yes," said Ruth decidedly, "we'd love to come, wouldn't we, Jack?" As Jack nodded, he caught Ralph winking at Priscilla.

"I think you'll find that you've never been to a party like it before," Ralph said.

Ruth was excited. "What kind of fancy dress do I wear?" she asked. "I've got nothing with me."

"It's easy," Ralph said. "It's a theme. Every party they give has a theme. Tomorrow night it's a game of chess. Wear anything, as long as it covers you completely, and it's all black or all white. One of you in each. Priscilla will give you a hand. The fancy dress part of it is only a formality. Come, let's go," he said, getting up to avoid further questioning. "I'll race you down the slope," he said to Ruth.

Ruth did not want to let Priscilla and Jack out of her sight. Slowly she followed him.

But Priscilla and Jack lagged behind. She took his arm again and they walked slowly down the slope. A monkey jumped out of the bush on one side, hopped in one leap across the road and disappeared into the bushes. "I don't know what to make of that guide of yours," Priscilla said.

"He's all right. He has his problems like all of us."

"D'you have problems, Jack?"

"Don't we all. Aren't we all trying to solve them all the time?"

"Some problems you don't solve," Priscilla said. "Some, you just have to grow out of."

"And how do you do that?" Jack laughed at her.

"You learn to compensate. You treat yourself occasionally."

Jack heard the seriousness in her voice. "Treat yourself? How?"

She stopped. They had come to a bend on the slope and no-one was visible. "I'll show you," she said. She clasped his head in her hands and pulled his face down to her lips. She kissed him with a hunger he would never have suspected and he noticed himself responding passionately, although her act had disgusted him. Another monkey crossed their path and disturbed them. They unlinked arms and walked on. It was another piece for Jack to fit in; even if it wasn't his it lay on the fringe of his pattern, an undistinguished background made up of parts of the same colour and almost the same shape, like the monotonous blue sky of his childhood jigsaws that he knew were the hardest to piece together.

On their way home from the point, Jack sat next to Ruth and felt very close to her. To Priscilla and Ralph, he felt vastly superior, and he included Ruth in his superiority. He knew the field Ralph and Priscilla were ploughing. He had been there himself, and it no longer held any attraction for him. To watch others at the game disgusted him. He pitied them both and wanted no part of them. It was only Ruth he wanted and he wanted to reach her via nobody.

## 16

They expected Jan soon after breakfast. He was going to take them to one of the native townships near Cape Town. But it was not Jan who came for them. Another guide, who introduced himself informally as Robert, explained to them that Jan had been sent on another assignment. He had sent his best wishes, Robert said, and hoped they would have a pleasant day. "On this trip," Robert added, "I'm afraid we can't take your friends." He had obviously been briefed by Jan. "It's a complicated business getting into a township and the fewer we are the better. Now, are you ready?"

They followed him to the car. Ruth was sorry that Jan hadn't come, and she felt partly responsible for his resignation. It was Ralph's fault really but she tried not to think of him.

Robert had borrowed Jan's car and the three of them sat in the front seat. They drove away from the beaches on the road towards the town. In daylight the no-man's land they had driven through on their first night was peopled with workmen, lazily moving bricks from one place to another, and pausing to watch each car as it passed by. Jack wondered whether the seal was still there, and as they passed the stretch of sand he raised himself in his seat and looked across the beach. It lay there still. Another attempt had been made at burial but the black snout had already eased itself out of the wet sand casing. No doubt they would re-bury it daily and the sea would disinherit it, until between the caresses of sand and sea, it would rot and disintegrate of its own accord. Since that night, Jack had had occasional doubts that he had seen the seal at all, and he didn't want to risk Ruth's confirmation. Perhaps the whole evening, the silence of no-man's land, the notice boards, the love and the seal on the sands, the beggar on the dunes – perhaps it had all been a self-induced nightmare. He was glad that the seal was still there. It proved the existence of his disordered jigsaw, and all the irrelevant pieces he had since acquired.

The road into the town was spotted each side with isolated shacks in the bush. Roofs of corrugated cardboard were visible in the occasional clearing and a whole construction of orange-boxes, wire netting and tin, haphazardly thrown together to cut off the bush on three sides. An African woman was draping a white sheet over a bush to dry and some children played in the folds of her skirt.

"Do people live in those shacks?" Ruth asked incredulously.

"Kaffirs do. That's the way they want to live," Robert said. "You wait until you see the township," he hurried on. It was an order to hold their fire until the other side of the picture had been examined.

They arrived on the fringes of the town. The district was a poor one with stretches of uniformed houses, slippered housewives, open doors, permanent wireless and vagrant dogs. A high grey wall ran along the edge of the road, and on it was written in black tar, ONE MAN, ONE VOTE.

"Look, Jack," Ruth turned to him, pointing it out. It was the first sign of protest they had seen.

Robert laughed. "Whoever wrote that is behind bars. Three years if he's a coloured man, less for the whites who ought to know better."

The length of the wall was spattered with the same slogan. "Your gaols must be pretty full," Jack said.

"We've got plenty of room for all of them. There are other things beside prison you know. Vote indeed. Most of them can't read, leave alone write. I tell you," he turned to them, "they'll have the vote when they're ready for it. In the Bantustans they'll have their own government. What more do they want?"

"Why don't you rub out the notices?" Ruth asked.

"Can't. Nothing'll get that stuff off. They're clever, those devils, but not clever enough."

At the end of the wall, on the corner, some rebel had managed before he was spotted to write ONE MAN. The police had made a fruitless attempt to erase it while it was still wet. It was smudged a little, but still legible. In his frustration the policeman had added WENT TO MOW, and although it was the most innocent of all the slogans on the wall the smudged writing at the end told the most subversive story.

"What sort of people write those slogans?" Jack asked.

Robert snorted. "Crackpots, if they're black, and if they're white they usually turn out to be Jews. And all of them are Communists. They ought to have a taste of Siberia, the lot of them."

Jack shivered and from the electrified tips of his hair to his trembling feet he felt personally accused. Yet he couldn't open his mouth. Perhaps he wasn't trying hard enough, he thought. Perhaps he could but he wouldn't. He felt a momentary hatred for the Jews in South Africa for causing him such personal embarrassment. Yet at the same time he felt an overwhelming sense of responsibility towards every single Jew in every part of the world and it made him furious. As furious as the notice boards had made him on the beach a few nights ago. He clenched his teeth, searching in his heart for excuses for his silence. And they obliged by crowding in. The man's stupid, you either kill him outright, or you ignore him. Or, don't say anything, Jack, you're a guest in this country. It's not your business. Or, in any case, what do they want to go and stick their necks out for? It'll be their turn next. This last excuse almost made him vomit. He couldn't allow himself to think like that. It was wrong, terribly wrong. If you didn't participate in the struggle you actively sabotaged it, and no decent man, Jew or otherwise, had the right to opt out. Yes, yes, he told himself, this is the right way to think. This is what I must tell this man, or kill him. But his mouth wouldn't open.

"Hitler knew a thing or two," Robert went on.

A last straw needn't break a camel's back. It can fracture it just a little and Jack's mouth slowly parted.

"We're Jews, you know, my wife and I," he said weakly.

Robert was not put out by this information. "Well, you're different," he said.

Jack didn't want to be anybody's pet Jew. "We're not different," he shouted, his jaw released at last, "we're all the same, and I tell you this, if I lived in this country I'd be writing on the walls too." Robert ignored him. The way this man and his wife looked and behaved only confirmed his opinion that Jews were the same all the world over.

Ruth squeezed Jack's arm. He smiled. For once, he was grateful for her understanding. In his mind an amorphous design was painfully assuming some semblance of shape. He felt ready to start assembling his jigsaw. If one shape was defined, the rest would follow. He looked at Robert and felt deeply grateful.

They by-passed the centre of the city and soon were out in the country again. The drive was long and monotonous. "Where do these people go to work, the ones in the townships, I mean?" Ruth asked.

"They work in Cape Town. Factories, domestics, road building, odd jobs."

"They come all this way, every day?" Ruth said. "We've been driving for hours."

"They have a special bus which we lay on for them," Robert said as if it were a daily charabanc treat. "Not just one, either, they run at regular intervals," he said.

"I haven't seen a bus yet," Ruth said, "and we've been ages on the road." Robert let it pass. He was not like Jan who desperately wanted his country approved. It did not worry him. In any case, it never occurred to him that there was anything wrong in herding thousands of people together, miles from their place of work, often cut off for years from their families because of the colour of their skin. To him it was right and proper. He had grown up with it, and he would no more have questioned it than he would a sunset. If people criticised it he thought they were simple minded and he was genuinely sorry for them.

The road wound endlessly and there were no signs of habitation anywhere. "Here we are," Robert said, slowing down the car. Ruth and Jack looked at the wilderness about them and as Robert turned the car to the right they saw hidden behind the bushes the silent beginnings of habitation.

Architecturally it was more refined than a ghetto. It had

no wall. It was fortunate in having its own natural screen in the green bush-land that muted its sighs and cut off its squalor from the road. The car swerved into the entrance. There was no gate. The township was an open prison. If you tried to get in or out after curfew all you had to contend with was the armed police in the sentry box and his two furious alsatians. The policeman raised his hand in salute as Robert slowed down the car. They exchanged greetings and news about families; Robert, the tourist-guide, was obviously a familiar figure at the township. Further up the road, a group of unarmed coloured policemen stood talking. They stood aside as the car approached and saluted. Robert ignored them and drove straight on.

The first houses, or rather shacks like the ones they had seen in the clearings outside Cape Town marked the beginnings of the township proper, and as if they were a signal the road thereafter degenerated into a dirt-track. Ruth gasped in horror. "It's not all like this," said Robert referring to the road as the car jerked up and down, "it gets a bit better further along. Perhaps you'd like to visit a family, heh? I've got one ready for you."

The location sprawled over a wide area of blocks of identical houses, separated by treeless tracks. In every front window, dead centre, stood identical Christmas trees, some half stripped, but most with the fresh bloom of never having been dressed at all. In spite of the thousands of inhabitants there was a pervading silence in the township. Silent groups clustered round the lamp-post-less corners and stared, whilst pot-bellied children silently strode the pavements dodging the imaginary lines.

The car pulled up at one of the houses and as it stopped women from the neighbouring front doors rushed out into the street with their families. The door of the house which was the object of the visit remained firmly shut, as if the occupant had been given strict instructions to wait for the knocking before making an appearance. As Ruth and Jack came out of the car, the crowds on each side moved in and silently stared at them. A little boy ran up to Ruth to touch the white linen of her dress. Ruth put out her hand to fondle his fuzzy black head, and as she did so she felt it was a patronizing gesture and she quickly withdrew her hand. It was painful that neither she, nor, she feared, the others could in this atmosphere accept the gesture as a natural one.

Robert went before them and knocked on the door. A decent interval elapsed, enough time to comment on the morning-rubbed brass knocker and the newly swept path, the clean darned net curtains on the windows. A woman opened the door and almost immediately her large family crowded behind her. Robert raised his eyebrows sternly. At the dress rehearsal, the day before, the family had been installed in the living-room at the front of the house, each casually industrious at certain tasks. The door was to be opened only by the mother to allow sufficient room for the guests to enter. Robert pushed his way in front and with one sweep of his arm scattered the human wall from the opening.

He strode into the hall. Ruth and Jack followed him. As they came into the parlour there was a sudden silence as the family raced back to their appointed tasks as if their teacher had unexpectedly appeared in the classroom. Robert had effected no introductions and Ruth was obliged to ask her hostess her name.

The woman chuckled. "Nkumba," she whistled through her white teeth. She turned and smiled coyly at her family and her shyness dissolved into a fit of uncontrolled giggling in which the adult members of the family joined. The children, to whom shyness was no embarrassment, stared at the white couple with blank joyless faces, puzzled by the laughter of their elders.

"Will you have tea, missus?" Mrs Nkumba asked Ruth. "I got it all ready," she said, pointing to the table, and she turned proudly to Robert as if confirming the fact that she had done her set homework.

"We'd love to," Ruth said. The artificiality of her politeness offended her. Everything she said and did, seemed to have the same artificial ring, yet she acted sincerely. If only she could achieve within herself sufficient freedom to be rude or polite at will. To be free enough to be honest, unencumbered by allowances for colour. She smiled at Mrs Nkumba, and felt guilty.

The children sat themselves eagerly around the table and the unaccustomed spread of cakes, jams and sweetmeats provided by the offices of the gold-mining company. Mrs Nkumba seated Ruth and Jack at the top of the table and as others of her family sat down she introduced them. All of them were cousins, except one; an exceptionally large woman who carried a baby on her back. She was Miriam, Mrs Nkumba's sister.

All the set places were now occupied and Robert, whom Mrs Nkumba in the safety of her own home had ignored, looked around for a seat. But not wanting to draw attention to his isolation he stood casually in a corner of the room and adjusted the lens of his camera.

Mrs Nkumba turned towards him. "Mister," she said with a giggle, "you work, and afterwards you will eat." She began to pour tea. Miriam's baby began to whimper and her mother unbuttoned the front of her dress. At the third button her right un-reined breast, pendulous as a tonsil, large and over-ripe, fell onto her arm. She took hold of it as if it were no part of her and flung it into the bowl of sugar in the middle of the table. Gently she eased it out and placed the black nipple, tabby with sugar grains, into the baby's mouth. Mrs Nkumba handed Ruth her tea and passed her the sugar bowl. Normally she did not take sugar, but in the circumstances she was loathe to refuse it in case her hostess imputed to her refusal some sense of distaste or superiority. In fact Miriam's action, natural as it was, had been distasteful to her and she wished again for the freedom to express it. She forced two spoonfuls into her cup. Jack refused the sugar. Ruth's acceptance had made it easier for him. He felt the black eyes around the table on him as he passed the sugar over. "We're Jews," he said.

He didn't really know why he said it. It had nothing to do with the sugar-bowl, yet he felt it painfully relevant. He'd often noticed, especially in his business, how non-Jewish friends had agreed with certain of his opinions rather than be accused of anti-semitism. It seemed to him that if you were a Jew or a Negro you could trust nobody, not even those you knew in other areas to be trustworthy. You were always one of someone's best friends. If you were a yid or a nig you ran the risk of being somebody's pet, you ran the risk of a grace and favour exclusion from your own people, you were offered a lie to live by and a betrayal to live with. "We're Jews," he said again, "my wife and I." And he felt it would eliminate the necessity of any further small talk between them.

Mrs Nkumba accepted it smiling. "We're like each other," she said, "your people and mine. We suffer," she giggled shyly, and the whole table put their hands over their mouths to suppress their laughter.

Jack had a fleeting feeling of resentment. It was all very well to make suffering a common denominator, but didn't the Jews tend to have a monopoly of that commodity? At least there were no gas-chambers in South Africa. He wondered whether he could allow the comparison. But what did it matter? Suffering didn't have to be equal any more than the pieces of a jigsaw. Some pieces would have to have priority or there could be no valid pattern. He would find a place for all suffering, whether of the pass-book or the incinerator. Both pieces were indispensible.

Meanwhile Robert was clicking away in his corner. Visually the scene was completely inoffensive and Robert would lie his own captions. He was ready to push off as soon as the tea was over. From the front door came sounds of voices and soon the room was filled with neighbours and their children who couldn't contain their curiosity any longer. They crowded round the table, staring at Ruth and Jack, and the Millars stared back at them; the two parties faced each other with overweening understanding, as a midget faces a giant on the circus grounds, each knowing with absolute certainty that the other is a freak. All were dressed in what was obviously their better attire, the Christmas Day clothing that they had clung to as if to hang on to the illusion of peace for ever. One of them, holding a baby in his arms, the child's full-blown belly nuzzling his nostril, sat down at the upright piano that stood against one wall of the parlour. He opened the lid and, gently weaning the baby's stomach from his nose, he handed it to the woman nearest him. Everybody, including Jack and Ruth, gathered round the piano as the man played a few introductory chords. A tiny naked Christmas tree, a bonus to the larger one in the window frame shivered on top of the lid and showered some thin green needles on to the keys. The man dusted them off as he played, and came to rest on a soft minor chord. He began to sing quietly, "Away in a Manger . . ." The others joined in with him and although they were many the aggregate sound was full, soft and tender. Ruth and Jack each careful not to look at the other joined in with them, ". . . no crib for a bed, The Little Lord Jesus laid down his sweet head."

At the word "Jesus" Ruth held her mouth shut. It was an unerasable hangover from childhood school prayers, and the belief that God would forgive your participation in the stranger's form of worship on condition that you didn't say the forbidden words. "Christ" and "Jesus" were words that would have stuck in a Jewish throat and were unspeakable, and the closed mouth was like a series of asterisks in an expurgated edition.

The choir grew more resonant and harmonically assured. Ruth joined in with gusto.

"The cattle are lowing, the baby awakes
But little Lord ***** no crying he makes.
I love thee, Lord *****, Look down from the sky,
And stay by my bedside till morning is nigh."

Ruth was suddenly aware of Robert standing behind her. He too was singing, drawn by the harmony and the sentiment, and momentarily oblivious of his company. Ruth turned round and smiled at him. Her smile underlined his instinctive act of communication, and he withdrew again into his corner.

Meanwhile, one carol merged associatively into another, and occasionally an authoritative solo voice pedalled the rest of the choir into a basic accompaniment. Jack found his arms linked with men and women at his sides, and he and Ruth were absorbed into the swaying movements of the singers. Occasionally a child would disengage itself from the choir and rush back to the table and the cakes that had been neglected, humming between spongy mouthfuls the glory of the Holy Child.

"We must go," Robert's gruff voice broke into an interval.

"Can't we stay a little longer?" Ruth asked.

"I've got another assignment," Robert said. He wasn't going to have them enjoying themselves.

"Another ten minutes?" Jack asked. He immediately regretted having asked this man a favour and Robert was quick to take advantage of his position of authority. He hesitated for a while, to give them the impression that he would allow a longer stay, then suddenly he said, "No, we must go back immediately."

Jack looked at him with hatred. Yet Robert too was part of his jigsaw, an unsubtle corner-piece, easily recognizable, belonging to the periphery, having no place in the central order of things.

Jack and Ruth took their leave of the Nkumbas and their neighbours and the whole street gave them a send-off into their car. As they drove out of the township into the white land Robert relaxed. "I didn't think your kind of people sang carols," he said.

Neither Jack nor Ruth answered. "Jews, I mean," he persisted, "they don't believe in carols, do they?" Jack shifted uneasily in the back seat.

"Funny sight, that," Robert went on, half to himself, knowing that he would get no response from either of them. "Blacks and Jews together singing carols." He chuckled to himself.

Jack raised his clenched fist and poised it, trembling behind Robert's cheek. Ruth stayed it in mid-air. She brought it down into her lap, and his fist tightened in her palm. He

176

caught sight of Ruth's finger-nails as she pressed them gently onto his hand. They were black and he thanked God for the security she was always able to give him. "For Christ's sake," he screamed at her, "why can't you keep your nails clean?"

# 17

Jack came back from the township raging with anger and with a desperate urge to piece together the fragments, large, small and elusive that he had accumulated. Again, he needed to be alone, but when he saw Ralph and Priscilla waiting for them on the terrace he remembered the party and he had a premonition that more pieces were to be found there. Like a field worker he had to explore every avenue of research before starting on his thesis. He would go to the party and after that he would be alone. He would opt out of the visit to the vineyards which had been arranged for the following day. He would politely plead fatigue due to the strong sun. He would spend the day alone in his room.

They had drinks on the terrace. Priscilla and Ralph were already equipped for the party, Priscilla in a shapeless white sheet and Ralph in a black dinner suit.

"What are you supposed to be?" Ruth asked.

"We're King and Queen," Ralph said. "We've got our crowns in the bedroom. You're supposed to go as knights, so Pris and I rigged up a couple of swords. Just dress like us and you're both fixed up."

"What d'you mean, *supposed* to go as knights?" Jack asked.

"The hostess likes to arrange the game beforehand. If everyone had their choice, they'd all go as royals, naturally.

You're lucky you weren't told to come as a pawn. That's a pretty difficult costume to rig up."

Jack rather resented being told how to dress. He didn't ever feel like a knight, not even in his day-dreams. He wouldn't admit it, but if he *had* to be ordered around he would have been happier as a pawn. He didn't see Ruth as a knight either, anymore than Priscilla a queen. The whole affair was a delusion. He felt a shiver on his back which by now he recognized as a prelude to the discovery of a new piece. He wanted to go quickly to the party, to get it over with, and at last to be alone. This need gnawed at him more and more, yet he feared that there was no end to his researches, that each avenue would lead to another, that only he, by an effort of will, could create the conditions in which his solitude could be ensured. He finished his drink and clapped the glass down on the table as a sign that he was ready to leave. "Well," he said, getting up, "shall we go and dress, Ruth?"

"What about the swords?" Ruth asked.

"I'll bring them down here," said Ralph. "See you in twenty minutes."

When they were alone on the terrace Ralph poured himself another drink. "You don't need to drink so much," Priscilla said, "Not for this kind of party."

Her observation irritated him and he refilled his glass.

"Why are you so nervous?" she asked.

"I hope we haven't made a mistake," he said, "inviting the Millars to this party. D'you think," he said, without looking at her, "that they're going to fit in?"

"Why do you have to discuss it?" she said angrily. She got up, patting the back of her hair. Ralph knew what she was doing even though his back was towards her. "You're quite right," he muttered to himself.

"I'll go and fetch the swords," she said.

"You might as well bring the crowns too," he called after her.

They drove to the party in the hired car and on the carriage drive, Ralph and Priscilla put on their crowns. A number of cars were already parked at the front of the house, and when Jack, armed with his wooden sword, walked towards the main entrance Ralph hissed to him to follow him to the side door. He put his fingers on his lips to ward off any questions that might be forthcoming. They followed to the side entrance. Jack noticed that the outside of the house was being painted. The pots of white paint and brushes were neatly stacked on the path. On the wooden support of the door hung a brass bell and this Ralph rang four times. After a short wait a small wooden panel in the middle of the door was slid open and a hand, holding four masks, two black and two white, appeared through the square aperture. Ralph accepted them and doled them out according to their matching colour. He whispered to Jack and Ruth that they were to put them on before entering. The masks practically covered the whole face. The eye slits were adequate for clear vision and occasional perforations in the mask itself allowed for sufficient respiration. Over the mouth was a hole to facilitate eating, and, when not in use, this was covered by a large flap. The faceless faced the faceless and confident in their new found anonymity they hurried excitedly to the front entrance.

An African servant opened the door. He was unmasked, yet his bland expressionless face could not have betrayed less had it been covered. He showed no curiosity in the new guests, as if all his life he had been opening the door to black and white masked uprights.

"Hullo, hullo," a lady screamed into the hall. She

arrived as her echo was dying away, smothering it with yet another screaming greeting like a fat lady vainly trying to obliterate her looming shadow.

She was a fat white bishop and in her hand she brandished a sceptre. Hanging from her immaculate smooth mask were two scraggy white chins like a hand-written postscript to a neatly typed letter. On her head she wore a mitre, which covered the dark roots of her blonde hair that strayed beneath the rim. She wore a long white dress that made a single concession to her identity. It covered her completely except at the breast area which was in major part revealed as two sunburnt semi-circles of time-worn flesh. Beneath the train of her dress were two satin high heels which, by her crippled gait, were giving her no pleasure. The white peep toes no more connected with the mitre on her head than her brazen bosom. She was an unmitigated lie from head to foot. She had, as Ruth later learned from other guests, come some years ago from England where she had been in "showbiz". When pressed for details she volunteered to her friends an acting career as understudy, stand-in, and prompter. Her "darlings" and extravagant gestures were imported hangovers from the wings of the English theatre.

She swooped down on Jack and Ruth like a clerical hawk. "No, no, no," she said, waving her white arms. "I don't know you. Promise, promise," she said coquettishly. "I've just come over to welcome you. Some knights at last, Paul," she crooned back over her shoulder into the room whence she had emerged. "Our first knights," she giggled. She stretched out her arms to Ruth and Jack in welcome. "They'll be two more. Two more," she wagged her head knowingly. "Just two," she laughed. "No gatecrashers at this party. I don't know whether I know you, really I don't," she reiterated her promise, "but in case we haven't met before, I'll tell you my name. It's the only name you shall be told,' she wagged her head mischievously. "Since I'm your hostess, we'll make one little exception. Vicki," she volunteered. "That's all I'm telling you. Vicki," she repeated in Ralph's and Priscilla's direction, though she had a shrewd suspicion that she knew that couple – Priscilla was patting the back of her head like a drum – it was a gesture with which Vicki was somehow familiar. "And that's all you need to know. Paul," she twittered as she turned to her husband who had joined her.

Though man he was, and a black queen at that, there was nothing about him to indicate his sex, and he evoked in his new guests a certain hesitation regarding it, like the hesitation of entering a field of cows and realizing that not all cows look female. His voice was gruff and low however and gave his guests some reassurance.

"Welcome," he said, and added rather pointlessly. "I'm Paul. You may know my name, too." After all, it was his name, he could do what he liked with it.

"Come in," he waved them into the drawing-room, again rather pointlessly because his wife was already leading the way, and he found himself straggling behind his guests.

Vicki was effecting the introductions. The guests were introduced not by name but by rank and allegiance. Those already assembled included the opposing black bishop, the white king and a scattering of pawns. The latter did not wear masks. Their faces were covered with black or white cloth hoods and they kept very much to themselves. Only one black rook was there, his rank distinguished by the limp South African flag he carried in his hand. He stood in a corner, isolated, waiting for other members of his regiment before he would lower his drawbridge and join the throng. Ruth heard the distant pealing of the side door bell. Three timid rings, and she guessed that three pawns were arriving. In the party's beginnings rank stuck to rank. Sceptre, sword and crown minded each their business while hooded pawns minded theirs. This latter group was shortly reinforced by three of their number, who, in their greetings, gave no indication of recognition. The side bell clanged again, with a peal worthy of a knight at least, and shortly afterwards more and more intermittent peals announced the completion of the game. Vicki greeted each new arrival in the hall, swearing on her heart that she couldn't recognize anybody. "You might even be my own mother," she screamed at the fat black bishop who was the last to arrive. The bishop joined a pawn in the drawing-room and at his initial move the whole structure of the society broke down and mask talked to mask indiscriminately. The four rooks still held their ground together. One of them carried a Russian flag, and Vicki teased him about it across the room.

"What does it matter, heh?" he said, coming over to her. "They're all the same. Coloured rags. As long as I've got something to wave, heh?"

The three remaining castles now mixed with other groups and the party became entirely mongrel.

Ruth was soon separated from Jack and when she looked around the room she couldn't find him. She looked at the men's feet, hoping to recognize Jack's patent shoes. But patent shoes seemed to be uniform. She wondered how it was possible to know a man so intimately and yet not be able to pick him out in a masked crowd. The thought frightened and excited her at the same time. She moved away from the king she had found herself with and she walked around the room leaning her ear to the various conversations. But even Jack's voice she could not recognize. She did the rounds a second time, guiltily whispering

"Jack?" as she passed each group. A hand suddenly clapped her shoulder. She knew it was a man's by its strength but she didn't recognize it as Jack's clasp. "No names," the voice laughed. "Strictly against the rules, heh? And what a charming knight you would make," he giggled again, "if I had the opportunity."

Ruth moved away from him. In her wanderings she had not even recognized Ralph or Priscilla. She cared less about not knowing them. It was the thought that Jack was possibly only a few steps away from her and that she did not know him. It was this thought that so disturbed her. She wanted to snatch off her mask and scream, "Jack" into the middle of the nameless crowd. She wondered whether he was looking for her, but everyone except herself seemed to be engaged in conversation. A black knight was coming towards her. It was Jack she was sure. She smiled at him beneath her mask. He had been looking for her after all. The figure came very close to her, put a hand on her shoulder and said, "Come and talk to me, my dear." It was clearly a woman's voice and Ruth shrugged her hand away and made for a group of pawns, who, mindful of their status, still doggedly stuck together.

She was reminded of a dream she had had shortly before they left England. There was a garden party and all the people were in gay dresses and quietly enjoying themselves, talking, eating, and laughing together. The guests glowed with the sun and with good company. Ruth had recognized none of their faces, but she too was enjoying herself. As she crossed the lawn to talk to a guest she woke up, sweating with terrible fear. The dream had been so peaceful and inoffensive, yet it had about it an indefinable quality of nightmare. She shivered with fear and the realization that she had no idea of what she was afraid, and for the rest of the night she had lain awake, trembling. This room, although seemingly quiet and respectable, had the same texture of horror for her. She longed to find Jack and feel his arm around her shoulder.

"Supper, my friends, whoever you are." Vicki's unmistakeable scream rang through the room, and the masks still in their groups made for the dining-room.

Through the slits in her mask, Ruth first caught sight of the floor. It was covered with black and white lino squares. The lino was worn in places and buckled at the seams. The floor had not been laid for the occasion. There had obviously been chess fancy dress parties at Vicki's house before. It was probably the perennial theme. Ruth wondered whether she was expected to place herself on any one square. She knew nothing about a knight's position on the board. She noticed however that people were standing about, still in their groups, with no reference to the tiles beneath them. In fact the dresses of some of the players masked the divisions of some of the squares, so that even an enthusiastic player could hardly have found his appointed place.

Had she not been masked, and the other guests too, Ruth would have felt very conscious of being alone. But in the general anonymity she didn't care. Her confusion and her self-consciousness couldn't show and if somehow it did, no one need know it was she. For after all, she thought to herself, what does loneliness consist of except the shame of its discovery by someone else. She began to enjoy being masked and to make grotesque faces to herself under the concealment. She wondered what all those people were like underneath it all. The timbre of a voice betrayed little, and the shrouded gait and draped gestures even less. Perhaps the purpose of the party was to discover the linings of the black and white shrouds that circulated about the room.

She made her way to the table that was laden with meats, salads and fruits of all kinds. Before helping herself, she watched the other guests eating, hoping to decipher Jack from his eating habits. But with features invisible all ate in exactly the same way, raising the black and white flaps over their mouths to shovel in a delicacy as if filling a boiler. She found this eating procedure disgusting but she indulged in it, nevertheless, confident that she was equally unrecognizable.

After the meal the guests returned to the drawing-room, and as if they had been through it all before they seated themselves along the side of the room. Ruth found herself next to a white hooded pawn. There were white slippers on the feet and the white dress touched the toes. She looked for an outline of breasts on the figure but could only make out a convex mound that could have been anything. Her ignorance of the figure next to her and of the assembly in general now made her feel infinitely sad. Sad that she should have become part of it. She felt her temples throbbing with despair and a hammering at the back of the skull. She hoped she would faint and although she gave herself completely to the hammering and the fever her mind remained clear. In fact her thoughts were of such new clarity she thought she was going mad, with the kind of dementia that leads to sanity. She shivered, winding her winding-sheet about her.

"Are you cold?" a simpering woman's voice leaked through the white hood by her side.

"No," said Ruth, "I'm all right." She was overwhelmingly grateful that the sex by her side had revealed itself. In the midst of the ghastly illusion it was a thread or reality to cling to. To be sure of anything in such a gathering was a miracle.

"Friends, whoever you are," Vicki was hollering in the

centre of the room. "Don't say I don't always have a little surprise for you," she shrilled. Her giggles dribbled from her mask. Poor Vicki had travelled six thousand miles to find a stage that could not deny her, and she was going to get back at least the cost of her fare. "Friends," she repeated, "whoever you are" – the joke, such as it was, was wearing a bit thin, and the guests could only manage a titter – "tonight, a little surprise." She paused. They had taught her at drama school that a pause lent weight not only to what had been said but what was to follow, and that particular lesson had struck home. Vicki's pauses were superb, and deserved follow-ups more worthy of them. "Hunt the thimble," she gasped in astonishment. The guests did not respond with much enthusiasm, apart from a single gasp of delight from one of them, whom Ruth assumed must have been Vicki's loyal Paul.

"Now the prize," Vicki went on and the guests listened with a little more enthusiasm, "the prize is a surprise," she laughed. "But this I'll tell you. The prize represents a diversion from our normal course of procedure. And not until the thimble is found," she wagged her finger dramatically – the gesture was from another lesson that had struck home. "When it is found," she went on, "I shall tell you what the prize is."

"Is it in this room?" a lady's voice filtered through one of the masks in the corner.

"Yes, it's in this room, this very room," Vicki shrilled. "And what's more, I'm going to help you." She paused again. In her own terms, something of import was going to follow. She dropped her voice to a whisper and leaned forward to her audience. "I'm going to tell you when you're warm," she confided. She straightened up again and said, "I shall tell you when you may begin." She was loathe to leave the stage and she paused a very long pause before her next line. "Now," she shrilled.

One would have expected a chaotic scramble on the part of the guests, but they rose leisurely and began a desultory search. Vicki still hogged the centre of the stage while her guests were equally distributed in the four corners of the room. After a while, one of the players noticed that almost the whole room was covered in the search and he shouted in an offended voice, "One of us must be warm, Vicki."

Vicki rocked with laughter. "Freezing, freezing," she screeched, "you're all freezing. Freezing," she said, remembering her lesson on the use and abuse of repetition.

The players gravitated to the centre of the room which was the only unoccupied area. Vicki moved away from them and watched their search from a corner.

"How are we now?" the same offended voice challenged her.

"Freezing, freezing," came her answer. "Like a glacier, the whole lot of you."

The players withdrew to the corners again and Vicki once more took the centre of the stage. "How about now, heh?" the voice was without any confidence. "I suppose we're freezing again."

"Like refrigerators," Vicki agreed. She liked to vary her similes. The players darted back to the centre and allowed no time for Vicki to move off-stage. They surrounded her as if they would devour her. "And now?" the voice thundered with more confidence.

"Warm," Vicki purred, "very warm."

The players were quick to cotton on to the whereabouts of the thimble. It was undoubtedly on Vicki's person. She certainly had given herself a starring role.

Some of the guests who were clustered round Vicki began

slowly to withdraw, and seat themselves around the room as if opting out of the game. It was clear, despite the masks and the winding sheets, that those who had withdrawn were all women who had no interest whatsoever in clambering over Vicki's body with a thimble as an excuse. Vicki had not only made herself the star, she had chosen the entire cast. Once again Ruth tried to decipher Jack amongst the black and white melée that probed the fat white bishop at its centre. But they had all gelled together, and like a grotesque octopus they wielded wild hands and feet about their quarry. In the middle Vicki held her ground, like a rock, solid as the establishment she represented. Her mitre had slipped sideways a little and she looked less like a bishop than a matey parson, but she stood firm, while her flock groped and probed and tickled her, like over eager customs officers making a private examination of a smuggler.

At last a man's voice called excitedly, "Got it, got it." With relief, Ruth recognized that the voice at least did not belong to Jack, yet in the atmosphere of imposture and delusion she could not be too sure of the body. The excited winner was clutching a fold on Vicki's dress, slightly above the abdomen. "Got it, got it," he kept shouting, though he had already made himself clear. The losers withdrew and the stage was empty, save for Vicki still standing firm like the Statue of Liberty with the winner grovelling in the folds of her dress like a new and grateful immigrant.

"Tell them the prize, Vicki," a man shouted from a back seat.

It was Paul. He, too, along with the women hadn't played the game, either because he knew where the thimble was, or, once given the clue, did not care to investigate. Vicki shrugged the winner off her person and he fell at her feet. He gathered himself together and stood up. He was a short thin man, a white-hooded pawn, and although as yet he had no notion of what the prize was to be, he was trembling with a mighty sense of victory and through the slits in his hood he eyed the defeated kings and queens with contempt.

Vicki waited for silence. Although the climax of her performance was past, she intended to give her all to the last. The guests had become restless, impatient to get on with the main business of the party. Although Ruth sensed their restlessness she did not know its cause, but she suspected that the climax of the party was yet to erupt. She looked around again for Jack, but not knowing him, she could only depend on his sudden hand on her shoulder and she wished it would come soon.

Vicki was ready with her pay-off line, and she intended to make a speech of it. "Friends," she started.

"Whoever you are," the guests chorused.

Vicki laughed generously. "Friends, I said at the beginning that with this prize we stray from the normal course of procedure." She paused. "Have you guessed what it is?" she asked.

The guests couldn't imagine. What Vicki called the normal course of procedure was abnormal enough, therefore if they were to stray from it they must somehow be back to normal.

"Something normal, is it?" a lady's voice asked.

"Something very normal," Vicki giggled.

"How infinitely dull," said one of the losers.

"We shall see," Vicki said with confidence. She turned to the little victor. "I'm so glad it's you, Wallace," she said. She clapped her hand over her mask, too late to smother the name she had divulged. A roar of disapproval rose among the guests. "That's certainly straying from normal procedure, heh?" said one.

"Apologies, apologies," Vicki said largely, distributing her arms around her guests. "The prize," she hurried on, "is as follows. The winner, whoever he might be, is tonight at this party, unlike at any of our other parties, to have free choice."

Little Wallace leapt in the air with glee and landed in the congratulations of his fellow guests. "Lucky devil. Make the most of it," they said. "Think it over carefully."

"I don't have to," he yelped with delight. "I know, I know. Is Alice here?" he yelled. "Where's Alice?" A black bishop stepped forward and willingly taking his arm, they left the room together.

Ruth was more confused than ever, and desperately she looked for Jack to see if he could offer some explanation. Jack on the other side of the room had understood what had happened and what was going to happen. He was glad he could not decipher Ruth from amongst the crowd and he fervently hoped she could not recognize him. He couldn't trust his mask to conceal his own personal excitement. "It's rotten, rotten," he cried to himself. "But it belongs here, in this rotting country, the lies, the swindles, the masterly self-delusions. It's rotten, rotten," and he tried to curb the surge of joy that crowded him.

"I think it's time for the parade," Vicki was centre-stage again. "Shall we line up?" she said. "The ladies to the left and the gentlemen to the right."

Ruth did not know whether she was referring to her own, that is, Vicki's left and right, or that of the audience, so she decided to follow Vicki, who was the only person in the room of whose sex she was absolutely certain. She found herself standing alongside her, against the book-lined wall, and, looking down her line, she was astonished at the tricks hood and mask could play with one's basic identity. Opposite shuffled an undisciplined line of masks; there were two black knights, but neither could she recognize as Jack. She wondered why they were lining up and she had a sense of excitement mixed with horror.

When the sexes had been officially separated, and no one could even be sure of that, Vicki left the line, and joined Paul in the gap in the centre, and facing each other, held hands above their heads. It was a signal for the lights to go out, and apart from the white robes and hoods Ruth could see nothing. What frightened her was the silence and the stillness, as if the sudden darkness had petrified them all; that they had indeed become wooden figures on a board, inanimate, without will. Stealthily she clutched her fingers under her heart and felt with relief its raging beat. She touched the figure alongside her, but it made no move. She prodded again, and again there was no reaction. She was suddenly terrified; she wanted to find her way out of the room, with or without Jack – it was by now largely a question of self-preservation – but she was afraid to move and disturb what was apparently the normal procedure. The silence was suddenly broken by Vicki's voice.

"Oranges and lemons," she sang shrilly. Her voice was on the outskirts of soprano, and she was joined by other members of the party, each in their own private voice range. The song sounded like a prayer, discharged in ecstacy, the choir transported beyond any notion of pitch. The singers soared and wailed and exulted in a fever of excitement, an accompaniment that was obscenely at odds with the innocence of the libretto. At the line "We owe you five farthings," a movement began, and Ruth felt herself turned by a pair of hands on her waist and automatically she clasped the waist in front of her. The line moved forward and the formless chanting and rhythmless steps fitted together like two amoeba momentarily caught in one mould. There was no hilarity in the game, nor any attempt to dodge the executions that awaited between the lines. At last the two tug-of-war teams were formed more or less equally on each side of Vicki and Paul. The chanting suddenly let up and the pulling began. Neither side pulled with a will to win; they seemed more concerned with soldering themselves together. Then, as if by previous arrangement, Vicki and Paul loosened their grip, and the two lines fell backwards in an orgy of scrambling and rumpling that went on in utter silence for several minutes and seemed to be the whole point of the game. Then the lights went on again and the two amorphous masses regained some shape and resumed their line-ups on each side of the room. Once again, Ruth tried to decipher Jack in the line opposite, but after the last game all symbols of rank had been abandoned, and it was impossible. She noticed that Vicki was not by her side, and she began to wonder whether she was in the right line. But her infallible shrill resounded from the dining-room. "The game, the game," she cried. There was a rush towards the door, but Vicki stood blocking the entrance. "Friends," she said – she omitted the corollary – "I wish you all you wish yourselves. There is a saying in my country, that each man wins what he deserves." (It was one of Vicki's fatuous ideas, but she thought that if she raised it to the status of an adage, her guests would take it more seriously). She giggled, and paused a pause. "May your deserts be your desires."

The party filed into the dining-room. The table had been removed, and a section of the black and white squares of lino had been cordoned off with ropes. An opening in one corner allowed entrance on to the board. On a make-shift platform at the end of the room, stood a table on which was a chessboard set for play. On either side of the table were two empty chairs. Below the platform stood the coloured servant who had opened the door to the guests. He clapped his hands for silence. "A black one," he called. An anonymous black figure stepped forward and the servant placed him on the rook's square in the corner. "A white one," the servant called again.

Ruth hovered in the waiting crowd. An overwhelming sense of doom filled her as the colours were called and suddenly she remembered Aba ben Saal and his prophesy of sad-dark after the chess game. She was tempted to scream "Jack" into the room to prevent him from entering the checquered arena. There was now no hope of tracking him down as a black knight. The servant was only interested in the colour of his pieces, and besides most of the signs of rank had by now been abandoned.

"And a white one," the servant went on. His voice was a sing-song; he called the colours as if he were calling the numbers in a game of Bingo. Ruth was now the only white piece outside the board, and she felt herself guided on to a pawn's square facing a line of black unknown.

Suddenly the lights in the room dimmed, and soft music seemed to issue from the walls. A spot light was thrown on to the chess board on the platform. Two players entered, one from each side and took their places at the table. Both were Africans and were dressed in evening suits. The servant who had set the board now moved into the centre of the game between the two lines of pawns, in order to manipulate the moves that would be called.

"Pawn to King 4," the first player called in a loud voice. The game had begun.

The servant repeated the move with the figures on the floor.

"Pawn to King 4," his partner replied.

The moves were called from the platform and executed below with very little pause for thought between them. It was as if the game had a pre-arranged pattern, all moves having been worked out beforehand.

"Knight takes King's pawn."

The servant at the centre moved the knight on to the pawn's square. A beam of spotlight centred on to the merged pair. They cancelled each other out and Ruth saw them vanish into the shadows, while the music, reinforced by one or two cymbals, congratulated them with a crescendo. Ruth shut her mind to what she already guessed was the purpose of the party. She felt that if she had to sin, it was more pardonable if she knew not that it was sinning, as an accused pleads diminished responsibility.

"Black knight takes white knight."

Ruth saw the unmasked Paul moved on to the Knight's square. His face bore no sign of curosity or excitement. Apart from the newcomers, he had, over the years, been through the whole guest-list. Nothing could any longer astonish or excite him. He was a tired man who had known it all and gained nothing.

The game proceeded. Each move ultimately led to the union of an unknowing pair.

"King takes pawn." There was a note of triumph in the player's voice as he called the move. He looked down at the guests disdainfully savouring the neat reversal of the status quo.

"King takes pawn," he repeated the move, winking at the servant who carried out his orders.

Ruth trembled in anticipation of her own move. All she could hope was that the masks would be kept firmly on until the whole purpose of the party had been achieved. In the dark and with the nameless, she could function. She might even find it enjoyable. But a disclosed feature of a face would freeze her; a wrinkled skin, or one youngly-covered with down, would humiliate her; any kind of disclosure would paralyse her with shame. She stood on her square, conscious of the one consolation of the game. It was not like musical chairs or a hurriedly improvised Paul Jones. You knew from the beginning that there was enough to go round for everybody. A wall flower at a chess party was an impossibility.

Jack, on his square, still awaiting his move, was not disturbed in the same way as Ruth. He hoped, on the contrary, that as soon as the game was over, the masks and the hoods would be put away and reveal all the ugliness that he knew must lay underneath. He knew that, except for Ruth who was not an habituée, there could not possibly be any beauty or decency under the masks. The habit of decadence must have corroded the flesh, and underneath the coverings everybody was even more hideously alike than when in disguise. It made no difference what fell to his lot. He could be certain that it would be foul and ugly. And the prospect of it excited him. Although Ruth needed the concealment and Jack the revelation, both of them needed the lie.

"Pawn takes pawn," the player called. The two guests met on the same square. Ruth saw the shoes, and realized with horror that both were men. The music again saluted their union, and wished them joy of each other.

As each figure stepped forward, Ruth wondered whether it was Jack. But even had she been able to pick him out, she would never have known what sort of parcel he had won in the lottery, or even what expression, whether of joy or disappointment, lurked behind his mask.

"Rook takes bishop," the orders came from headquarters. An old man was pushed forward. He was very lean and he walked slowly and with a stoop. He had hung on to his sceptre, which he now used as a stick to support him. Unlike the others he was still neatly dressed with his accoutrements intact. He had probably given the slip to the parlour games that had preceded the lottery and had only joined in for the serious business of the evening. He was the booby prize of the game and must have been close on a hundred. He tottered on his square and waited for his unfortunate partner to cancel him out. His intended partner was seen to shudder at the wretched bundle on the square, no doubt salivating in expectation under his mask, and the figure stepped forward, trembling, to meet him. Such was the luck of the draw. A murmur of pity went up through the remaining guests on the board. He took his partner's arm, needing support, and the figure led him slowly into the shadows.

Ruth was relieved when her move finally came. She felt herself directed on to a square, and a tall figure came to meet her. She let herself be led away, ashamed of the excitement inside her.

"Pawn to Queen 7," the player called with finality.

The music offered its last compliments, and the room suddenly slipped into darkness.

There was a sudden great noise of movement on the floor. Ruth felt her partner, pulling her downwards, until she was lying on the hard lino, with groans and movements all around her. In the small light that filtered through the window, she saw around her, like a black rough sea, a sprawling shrouded mass, she saw the servant and the two master players turn aside on the platform, leaving the confusion they had created, wallowing in its own anarchy. Then and there, on the black and white floor, the sickness of the state would spread. At their bidding, the king would fraternize with his subject, and knight would consort with knight. The bishop would take his queen and the pawn would enter the castle. The natural order would be destroyed.

Jack fondled his partner's body beneath the shroud. He had an insatiable desire for whatever horror lay hidden beneath. He felt her responding body and it nauseated him into a greater lust.

"Are you free now?" a voice whispered from one side of the floor.

"I'm available," another offered.

Jack covered his partner with his own shroud, and as he did so, he felt the body beside him move into the space he had vacated. In the movement the figure had pressed on Jack's side, and Jack could not help but transfer the pressure to his partner.

"Oh please," she called out, "you're hurting me."

In cold horror, Jack recognized the voice as Ruth's. He shivered. At the thought of her naked face and body, all desire for her evaporated. He staggered to his feet and walked away. It was not a husband leaving his wife's side; it was one false witness parting with another. His body limped with terror, and he stumbled over the figures on the floor till he reached the door. He tore off his mask, and an old coloured servant-woman stared at him pityingly.

"Will you have something to drink, master?" She was old, his mother's age, had she been alive, fat and round, and compact as an envelope. He felt the familiar shiver on his back and he trembled at her ugliness. Not only had he found a new piece, but he knew its shape, its colour and its centrality. To possess it was vital to his jigsaw; without it he would be forever inadequate. The hangover rage from the township quickened his desire for her. He did not see her eyes, startled that he had not answered her, and he did not hear her ask the question again. He only saw that she was old, black, and forbidden, indeed, so riddled with impediments, that he could truly love her.

"Do you want anything, Master?" the old woman asked again.

He wanted her, and he had to steady himself against the wall to stop himself from taking her by force. "Please go away," he pleaded as gently as he could.

The woman shrugged her shoulders and went down the hall, and Jack managed not to follow her. She was a piece he would have used at his peril.

He staggered to he front door, frightened at a brewing violence inside him. He gave no thought to Ruth. He wanted to get away from the sad decadent despair of them all. "I don't want any of you," he screamed back at the door. "I hate you all," though it was himself he hated more than anybody. "You disgust me," he hissed. He wanted to kill them and all the rottenness inside him. He felt a furious need to destroy and it was uncontrollable.

He found himself running from the house. He saw himself pick up a pot of paint and a brush from the gravel path, and he ran down the street, panting after his own footsteps, trying to shed the rage inside him. He didn't hear the two policemen following him for they drowned their steps in his. He reached the end of the street, and the high brick wall that sealed off the corner house. He put down the pot of paint and hurriedly dipped his brush. He poised it on the wall, catching his breath, while the white paint dripped down his sleeve. He was less concerned with what he would write than with the neatness of his hand. He had a clean wall and a bright white brush and he had to do his best writing. He curled his tongue round his upper lip, and as he wrote the fury drained out of him.

The two policemen had stopped on the opposite corner, from which point they had a splendid eye-full of the proceedings. They followed the sweep of Jack's brush as he painted with meticulous care. ONE MAN COMMA, the wall sang out, ONE VOTE. Jack took a step back to view his work. He realized that what he had written was not the root of the matter at all. What had happened inside him, with the old black servant woman, that was the heart of things. Writing it down was only second best, but at least it was a way of getting it out of his system.

He approached the wall again and stood on his toes. The voting issue was secondary and had to come after the main point had been established. High on the wall he wrote with a confident hand, MISCEGENATION IS THE ONLY SOLUTION. The writing was none too neat and he was not too sure of the spelling but the message was clear. He was satisfied. He looked at his wall again and decided to enclose his personal protest in inverted commas.

The police allowed him this finishing touch, then, beaming with the prospect of promotion, they crossed the road. One of them turned to the other and said, his seams bursting with his IQ. "We've got a case, heh?" They grabbed Jack and, pulling him between them for a larger share of the catch, they dragged him back the way he had come. Jack managed a backward admiring glance at his signwriting. The inverted commas gave the message a certain prestige.

On his way to the police-station, and possibly to the solitude he had so long craved for, he had an almost uncontrollable desire to see Ruth and to love her. Back in England, whenever he had left his mother's house or Carol's flat, he had felt the same kind of desire, as if his mother and Carol had been a rehearsal for what was really important to him. A third party was a springboard to Ruth, waiting, hoping and loving.

He turned to the policemen. "I must see my wife," he said.

"You can telephone her from the station."

Jack suddenly remembered how he had left her on the floor and he shivered with the recollection of the horrors of the evening. He realized he would be alone, and Ruth inaccessible. His latest third party hadn't paid off at all. It was as if, after a successful dress rehearsal, the play had been abandoned.

PART FOUR

## 18

The morning papers in England comfortably carried the story of the Millar's visit to the township. It had to rely on scenery description to cover up the lack of printable comment from the Millars. The whole article was in fact a re-hash of a South African government hand-out to tourists on the picturesque advantages of separate development. An account of the Millar's visit to the vineyards was wearily promised for the next day and its source would no doubt be a similar official hand-out. But the following morning when the reading public turned to the usual page to follow Ruth and Jack's vincultural adventures they read that the Millars in South Africa article was held over due to pressure on space. Its usual middle-page spread was devoted to a valuation of recent pop records. One morning paper carried a half an inch suspicion of Mr Jack Millar's doubtful adventures, but by the evening the story had broken and the wall-daubing Millar landed on every front page.

Jack Millar was charged under the National Laws Further Amendment Act. The judge took into account, or so he claimed, the nationality of the defendant and his unfamiliarity with the laws of the country. On the other hand, the context of his sign-writing implied a positive awareness of certain laws, so a formal deportation order was out of the question. He, therefore, in his wisdom, such as it was, sentenced him to six month's imprisonment which was the sentence he would have received if charged under the Immorality Act. Such a man, the judge said, capable of publishing obscene opinions, was capable too of putting them into practice. Such a man, here or in any country for that matter, was dangerous on the loose. "Six months," the judge repeated, and he tugged at his gown with righteous indignation.

The court room had been reasonably empty. Mural painters were a daily occurrence in the dock and the trials and sentences varied only according to the colour of the artist. Ruth sat on an empty bench a little way behind the dock. Jack would not have wanted her to face his humiliation. Neither Paul nor Vicki nor the Summers had come to the proceedings. There was no question that they did not know about Jack's arrest. Ruth had told the Summers at breakfast at the hotel, but they already knew from Vicki and Paul who had seen it in the morning paper. Ruth was relieved that they had not come. They were probably terrified that Jack might divulge the circumstances which had led to his nocturnal adventures. No doubt they were at this moment together somewhere, dissecting last night's party and salivating over the outcome. It would not occur to them that Ruth knew no-one in the town and was in dire need of support and companionship. They were the sort of friends who would come to your funeral only if they were guaranteed a party afterwards.

After sentence had been pronounced on Jack, he was taken from the dock to the cells below. Ruth hurried from the court room and down the stairs to see him. He was waiting for her between two warders.

"Only a few moments," one of them said. He stood aside as Jack caught Ruth in his arm. "Please don't try to understand me," he pleaded with her.

"I love you, Jack."

"Keep loving me, please," he said. "I'm not sure why I did it. You do things and find reasons for it afterwards. Let *me* find the reasons, Ruth. Just wait for me. I'm only sure of one thing," he cradled her face in his hands, "when I come out, I shall be ready for you."

He seemed already to have come to terms with his sentence, and Ruth was angry at his willing acceptance. "I'll go to the Consulate," she said. "It's an impossible sentence. I'll get you out. Don't worry. Just be patient, I'll do everything." She wanted to get away quickly to accomplish his release. "Don't cling to me like that," she said. "It's not going to be very long." She kissed Jack hurriedly. She did not want a dramatic parting. She had the utmost conviction in the reversal of the sentence, in the fact that the judge had made a terrible mistake for which he would no doubt be very sorry. "I'll see you very soon," she said with confidence. "The whole affair is quite ridiculous."

Jack watched her as she ran up the steps. In a way he was looking forward to being alone. He had so many thoughts and plans to put in order, and although he wanted to be with Ruth, he half hoped that her mission would not succeed.

# 19

It was fortunate that Jack's father was on a business trip abroad when the story broke, and the avalanche of reporters were obliged to traipse across London and descend on the Lazarus household.

Grandma, who had moved in for the crisis, kept them at bay. One or two had resorted to the telephone, wanting tit-bits of the sinner's background. One of them wanted to know whether Jack had ever played cricket. Grandma had long pondered on the relevance of that enquiry.

Mr Lazarus had taken the day off work to comfort his wife who had taken the news badly.

"A writer he said he was," Mr Lazarus moaned. "Such fancy words he uses. Why, even his own mother-in-law doesn't know from them the meaning." Her two sons, though secretly proud of Jack, tried to comfort her.

The door bell rang and Grandma went to open the door. A man stood there, a briefcase in his hand. Grandma recognized the signs of office and she half shut the door. "We are out to newspapers," she said.

"But I'm from the *Yiddish Monthly*."

That was different. Grandma opened the door to invite him in. You couldn't shut the door on your own people, and in any case, it was not their business to splash the story, but somehow or other to cover it up.

"It's all right, everybody," she shouted into the kitchen. "It's the *Yiddish Monthly*."

The man followed Grandma into the kitchen, where he sat himself at the table, very much at home.

"A cup of tea I'm making," said Mr Lazarus, going to the stove.

"It's a bad business," the reporter said.

"You won't write about it?" Mrs Lazarus pleaded.

Her husband came back to the table with a tray. "You won't be printing it?" he said.

"Mr Lazarus, it will be in all the papers," the man said heartlessly. "*The Monthly* has to say something too. The point is and that is why I'm here, what are we going to say, and how are we going to say it?"

"But you don't come out till next month," said Mr Lazarus hopefully. "By then, all is forgotten."

"Such news," said the reporter with relish, "is always news."

"If you're so determined to print it," Mr Lazarus said disdainfully, "it doesn't matter how, does it?"

"We can soften it a little," the reporter said.

"For instance?"

"The boy's parents are Jewish?" he asked.

"Natural," said Grandma, offended.

The reporter sensed there was no help coming from that quarter. He turned to Mr Lazarus. "You're Jewish, Mr Lazarus, of course."

"Of course, I'm Jewish."

"And you, Mrs Lazarus?"

"Such a question," Grandma moaned.

"Your father Mr Lazarus was also Jewish, through and through?"

"My father was the rabbi of Pinsk," Mr Lazarus said proudly.

"A rabbi?" The reporter was put out by the news. "Too bad," he said. "And your parents, Mrs Lazarus?"

"Also," said Grandma, seeing no more relevance in his line of enquiry than the question concerning cricket.

"Is there *no-one,* in your family or the boy's family," the man persisted, "either side, your side, your wife's side," he was giving them every opportunity, "is there no-one who *isn't* Jewish?" He was desperately seeking a loop-hole, groping for some non-Jewish family strain that would account for Jack Millar's aberrations.

Mr Lazarus finally saw what he was getting at. In the presence of other people, he was a man of few words, but suddenly, faced with the man's obscene investigations, he found himself choking with argument and indignation.

"Mr Reporter," he said, standing up. He had no idea of what he was going to say, but he knew that his mouth was full and in order that he should be intelligible, he had to empty it slowly. "Mr Reporter," he repeated, "if someone, for instance, gets the Nobel Prize. His name is Smith; he is educated perhaps in a Baptist college; his father is a vicar. Yet he gets the Nobel Prize. And you," he spat out, "and people like you, you break your neck to find him a Jewish grandmother. If some Tom, Dick or Harry, for instance," he went on, "suddenly becomes Sir Tom, Sir Dick, or Sir Harry, again you run to Somerset House, you should find for them a Jewish booba. Mr Reporter," Mr Lazarus said calmly, "in our history, people have been to the gas-chambers for having Jewish grandmothers." He paused. He hadn't remembered what he'd said, and he had no idea of what he was going to say, but Jack's predicament had given him a sudden feeling of relief.

"Yes," he went on slowly, "my son-in-law is a Jew, through and through, as you say. What he has done is not a Jewish thing, is not a non-Jewish thing. An ordinary human thing he has done, my son-in-law." He sat down.

The boys applauded, and Grandma smiled at her son-in-law. She was proud of him. She turned to stare at the reporter.

The man sensed the group's hostility. He rose to go. His visit had been fruitless. He had no idea what copy he should turn into his paper, and he decided to give it the slip altogether.

When he had gone Mrs Lazarus started crying again. "Poor Ruth. D'you think they'll keep him in prison?" she asked, as she had asked many times before.

"There's nothing we can do, Chayala," Mr Lazarus said. "We must just wait and see." He tried to recapture the pride and confidence he had felt during the reporter's visit. But in the back of his mind he had to admit to himself that it was shame his son-in-law had brought upon him. It wasn't Jack's protest against the system that angered him. It was his solution to the problem that offended him. It just wasn't right. He watched his wife crying silently into her handkerchief, and he had to fight down a growing hatred for Jack.

"Go and do your homework," he screamed at his sons. "What d'you think this is. A holiday?"

# 20

In his cell, Jack was glad to be alone. Right through the short trial, he had known the outcome, and so desperately did he need his solitude, that he would have volunteered to be sentenced without the paraphernalia of the mitigation plea. He had no hope of Ruth's attempts to obtain his release, but he was glad she would have something to occupy her time. Now he was alone. Even if it was only for a week or so before he would join others of the sign-writing and colour-blind fraternity, he would have time, time to order his past life, and from the pattern, design a future.

He looked around him. At first glance he knew that there were few enough focal points in the room on which he could concentrate, and he felt perhaps that he would have too much time. He examined the room slowly, corner by corner. In the further corner by the door there was nothing. The area was so empty that Jack crouched down into it, spreading his arms against the adjacent walls for balance. He spread his knees to touch each wall, smiling, feeling the corner full. He decided he would never look into that corner unless he was inside it. He rose slowly, turning his back on the wall, and counted his steps to the opposite corner.

In it stood a bucket. He bent down and outlined its shape with his fingers. Never before had he been concerned with the shape and texture of materials. Even though he worked in the rag trade he *saw* what was velvet and what was serge. He would touch and finger it because others did likewise but he had never found pleasure or discrimination in the touch. The grey zinc of the bucket was cold, and if he scratched it with his fingers it sent a shiver through his body. The inside of the base was stamped with concentric circles raised a little on the surface, and these he strummed gently like a harp. He was pleased with this corner. It was profitably and aesthetically filled. It would help him put his mind in order. He looked at the bunk near the opposite wall, and walked diagonally across the room towards it. He tested it with his hand. There was no spring but a sad sagging that seemed unwilling to rebound. A single blanket covered the bunk. Jack sat down and pulled the blanket over his shoulder. He wondered what kind of man had inhabited it before him. He smelt the grey fibres but a patchy smell of carbolic had erased most of the clues. Here and there, however, the former occupant still smelt through. Jack lay down on the bed and covered himself with the blanket. He wanted to get inside the former tenant, to try the man on, to discover if he had bequeathed him some form of friendship, some mark, some sign that he had been here and survived. He sniffed about him, like a dog hot on a scent. Here and there he caught the odours of the man's formula. He smelt the sudden surprised sweat of a man who ordinarily sweated but little. Of a man who, in his unbuttoned days had rarely been afraid, had rarely known acute joy or despair, but who, with the sudden onset of all these things, was equipped only with his sweat to express them. The "whys" that has so often stuck in Jack's throat must have vomited from his predecessor's and left their stench on the blanket. Here and there the fibre had been worn ragged with tooth-prints of despair, and the woollen threads had been rubbed thin for company. He sheathed himself completely in the blanket, and taking deep breaths, smothered himself in the fumes of loneliness, the loneliness that smells, like love sometimes smells or a house of mourning. He shrugged the blanket off him and laid it neatly on the bunk. This, too, was an occupied corner of the cell. That made three corners that he could without difficulty cope with.

He was relieved to find that the fourth corner of the room was occupied too. He strolled across the room to examine its contents. A water-closet, fully-plumbed and fitted. The bowl was clean and the water inside. There was no seat, but it had an S-bend, a tank and a chain. Jack pulled on the rubber ball. There was no response at all. Yet he was not disappointed. He was just grateful that the corner was occupied and had a semblance of luxury. He had a sudden desire to use the pan, together with the astonishment that, being in prison, the normal functions of a human being should still visit him. And with the realization came the knowledge that perhaps sometimes he would want to cry too, to make love, to die.

He paced the width and length of his cell, measuring and counting his steps in order to find the exact centre, and there he stood, six foot by one, in the middle of his cell. He was acutely concerned with symmetry and this central positioning of himself was part of his zeal to put things in order. He stood erect, wiping out the folds of his prison uniform so that no creases should disturb the clean pattern. He stretched out his left leg, like the arm of a compass, and swivelled around on his right, delineating a circle on the floor around him. This space he decided to reserve for his jigsaw. It would be somewhere to go, a little walk from the bed in the corner of the room. It would be almost like going to work every day, and if he took tiny steps and made a detour or two around the water-closet in the other corner, it might even take as long.

He was suddenly stabbed by the futility of his arrangements and he felt a mounting panic inside him. The silence of the cell terrified him and he stuffed his fingers into his ears to see if it were absolute. But with his ears covered the silence was intensified and when he uncovered them he knew that the cell was not quiet at all but filled with the hum of idle habitation. He looked around the cell and saw it no longer as four occupational corners with a study at its centre, but as five separate prisons of his own creating. He saw himself as the prisoner of them all, isolated and afraid. He knew that he was turning pale because of the fever he felt inside him. He noticed that his nails were picking at his hands and arms, as if his entire skin was yet another prison that confined him. He had a feeling that he would melt with fear and he stiffened himself up against the wall. Above all, he must hold back his vomit. He clutched at the sides of his head while despair stampeded his entire body. He felt tears on his face and as the panic burst inside him he screamed aloud. A long uninterrupted scream of pain and fear and the injustice of it all. He crawled over to the cell door shrieking aloud.

"Let me out," he screamed, tearing at the door with his hands. "It's a mistake. Let me out." He clambered up to the door, howling the error of his confinement and he took to banging at the door with his fists. "Let me out." He was astonished at the volume of his voice and heard it pierce the cell walls. Even as his cell door opened he went on screaming, as the full meaning of his whereabouts became clear to him.

"I was waiting for your outburst," the warder said. His voice was gentle. He had seen this kind of display hundreds of times before. Panic in a prison was never silent or well-bred, and the best of them threw off dignity in despair.

"Get up," he said sympathetically. "Everyone goes through this sort of thing in the beginning. You took a little longer than most," he observed. He guided Jack towards the bed and sat down beside him. He laid his hand on Jack's knee and Jack was half-grateful for the touch. "You've got six months to do," he said. "After a week you'll be with the others and it won't be so bad. And there'll be exercise and you can get out into the sun." He smiled, and after a pause he said, "And I'll come in from time to time to visit you."

Jack shifted his knee from the man's hand. He stood up quickly, trying to hide his revulsion.

"You've got six months," the man was saying, more for his own benefit than Jack's. "Settle down. You can do a lot of thinking in six months. Make plans for the future. That sort of thing."

Jack wanted the man to go. "I'll manage," he said. "I'll manage on my own," and he walked to the door as if to put an end to his hospitality.

The warder came across and put his hand on Jack's shoulder. "It's surprising what a man can get used to," he said

The remark rang through the cell after the warder had gone and Jack shuddered at its offensive ambiguity. He dreaded another visit from his keeper and he dreaded too the idea of exercise and his inevitable company. Outside the cell door, or inside, he was trapped. He was terrified, but he couldn't even scream any more. He sat on his bunk gripping the iron frame and he thought of Ruth and wanted her. He could cry silently and try with his tears to dissipate his despair. But his eyes remained dry. He lay back on his bed and felt a burning behind his eyes. It was better that way. His sobbing was silent and invisible. Only he would know the churning heartache inside him.

# 21

After her interview with the Consulate Ruth was offended at his lack of indignation. She herself was so incensed at Jack's sentence that in her opinion even a war between the two countries would have been justified. The man who dealt with such matters when they occasionally arose had raised an eyebrow at the story, which in diplomatic circles was the official movement to express Her Majesty's displeasure. "We'll do all we can," he said mildly, "though it will take some time."

"I'll wait," Ruth said, sitting down.

"Madam," the man smiled. "It may take a week or more before anything happens, and even then I can make no promises."

"Then what shall I do?" Ruth said helplessly.

"We will keep you informed, Mrs Millar. You must let us have your address." Ruth did not want to give them the hotel. She had decided to move closer to the Consulate. "I'm not quite sure where I'll be staying. I'll come in every day."

The man shrugged his shoulders. "As you wish," he said.


Ruth went back to the hotel to pack their bags. They were

already packed and waiting in the hall. The manager gave her a sympathetic glance and sent a boy for a taxi. "Those were my orders," he said, eyeing the luggage. "There was nothing I could do. They came an hour ago and saw that it was done."

'They' were the representatives of the Bokfontein Mynbou Maatskappy Beperk who had footed the bill for the first two days while Mr Millar had behaved himself, but who saw no reason to finance a prolonged stay. As far as they were concerned, the Millars were a bad debt and they wanted to forget about them. They would replace their London representative and insist on a detailed dossier of all future recipients of their generosity.

Ruth found a small boarding house near the Consulate. The landlady was a kind old woman who asked no questions, and Ruth stifled a desire to tell her everything. She gave Ruth a key with a large tab on it. "Room 14, my dear," she said. "Second floor."

She went over to the dressing table and pulled out the drawers. Each drawer was lined with old sheets from the *Cape Times* newspaper, with headlines of violence on each page. Robbery, assault, murder, immorality, and one or two apologetic pending-trial suicides at the bottom of the page. In the top drawer the last tenant had left a rusty razor blade. Ruth shut the drawer quickly. Through the slanting mirror she could see the door of her room lean towards her, and when she turned around the wardrobe door creaked open. She trembled. She had the feeling that someone else was in the room, that the former tenant had not completely left, that he or she had left behind in the empty drawers, the ill-made wardrobe and probably on the sagging bed, some shavings of loneliness that in side-street unchristened hotels take up permanent tenancy. She thought of Jack and hoped that he was sleeping. For a moment she acknowledged their six months separation, and grabbing a handbag she rushed from the room.

## 22

Jack had been in prison for six days, and each day had passed with the confirmation of his decision to put his life in order on the following day. He knew he could delay it no longer. Ruth was working for his release and if she were immediately successful he would have achieved nothing. He moved decisively to the centre of his cell and sat cross legged on the floor. He recalled the pieces of his jigsaw and wondered how he should make a start. He knew that he had to begin with a piece, the shape and colour of which he was absolutely sure. Yet he knew that the shape of each piece could not be fashioned independently, that its fitting must depend on the shape of the others, that the shape and colour of a piece was quite arbitrary, until it called for juncture with another. About the seal, he knew the most. It was round, black and sagging with impotence. The black figure of the woman servant to whom he declared his love in white paint was its neighbour only in colour, but its shape was alive and potent. He momentarily disjoined the ill-fitting pieces and placed them on one side. He thought of the notice board on the beach, Jan, the monkeys, Robert and his Jews, Ralph and Priscilla. He remembered the enthusiasm with which he had seen them all as a part of a single pattern; now he saw no relation between them whatever. They were like single items in a list of lost property.

He tried not to think of Ruth. He ached to be with her. He ached for any kind of unobserved company.

He heard someone coughing. The sound seemed very close, and he raised his head, hoping it would come again. And it did, twice in succession, with a short pause, followed by a long spluttering. It was as if a larynx was working the morse code. He waited, excited, anticipating company. "Hullo? Hullo?" the voice said. He jumped up. "Hullo." he shouted. He waited. "Hullo," he tried again, not knowing where to direct his voice. "Hullo." He tried a whisper.

Still no answer. He sat down on the bed again. He wanted a friend very badly. The coughing startled him again. He nosed round the cell trying to locate the sound. It was somewhere in the area of the lavatory, but it had stopped before he could pin-point it. He decided to sit on the pan and wait. Somewhere around him, in the floorboards or through the wall, somebody was trying to make contact. He thought of Ruth again, or rather, he thought of his wife, because for a moment he couldn't remember her name. This worried him a little, but he set it aside, knowing that later on he would recollect it. He heard the coughing again, a faint introductory cough as if it were to be followed by a speech. He strained his ears, listening. ' Hullo," a voice roared out. The greeting resounded underneath him, and he jumped off the pan. He knelt down and leaned his ear close to the enamel rim.

"Madalena," the voice shouted. It was a name that fitted snugly into the S-bend of the pipe. The caller let it run its course through the bend, then shouted again. "Madalena." The syllables gurgled through the pipe and echoed through the cell. "Lena, Lena," sang the bucket and the bed, and the empty corner wailed its lonely echo. If there were a sound of love, Jack thought, it would be Madalena, and if there were a shape, it was an S-bend. He listened for the voice of love to answer. There was silence. "Madalena," the suitor called again. Jack sensed his disappointment as the last syllable drained down the curve. Perhaps the man would be satisfied with some answer, even if the wrong number replied. "Hullo," he said into the white pan, in as friendly a voice as the conditions would allow.

"Who's that?" the caller said with angry indignation. "I want Madalena."

Jack knelt forward and stared into the pan, as if he expected Madalena to materialize from the white enamel. There was a preliminary hum and her voice came through, low-pitched and grating.

"Joseph," she said.

"Huh," Jack muttered contemptuously, "a pretty poor name for an S-bend." Then he realized sadly that his own monosyllable appellation would hardly make the first loop.

"Madalena," the caller said. Contact had been established. "Tell me again what you look like, Madalena." This message, together with its echo took quite a long time to get through.

"Big, big, big, breasts," the voice roared through the bend, hovering sensually on the reverse camber. Jack trembled. "Ruth, that's what she's called," he remembered. He felt tears in his eyes and a melting in his knees. He hoped the conversation would continue, though he knew he could hardly bear it.

"And the nipples?" the caller asked, after having swallowed the last answer.

"Black, black swords," Madalena obliged again.

How well did Joseph know Madalena? Jack thought. He'd obviously never seen her. Yet over the yards of prison plumbing he orgied himself on her anonymous anatomy.

Somehow he had initiated a pen-pal correspondence through the prison lavatory-system. It was in its beginnings, the exchange-of-photographs stage. Jack was glad he had come in so early on in the course.

It took Joseph quite a while to digest this last piece of information. Jack thought he heard him swallow.

"And the belly?" his voice trembled through the pipe. "Oilysmooth, smoothoily," Madalena knew how to satisfy her clientele. The words undulated through the bends, gently throwing an echo against the cell walls, where, caressed, it returned to Jack's trembling knees. For such a performance the accoustics of the cell were superb.

"Oilysmooth, smoothoily," Jack's knees were crumbling with the sound. This last rejoinder of Madalena was obviously enough or too much for Joseph. There was a long pause, Joseph repeating the words rhythmically to himself, like a lover reading and re-reading a love-letter. Jack decided to take advantage of the interval. By the sound of Madalena she had enough solace for both of them.

"Hullo, Madalena," he whispered familiarly, into the pan. He pointed his voice to the left, in Madalena's direction. He didn't want Joseph to hear his trespassing.

"Get off my line," Joseph yelled. He might have been momentarily satisfied, but he was mindful of his future needs. He had obviously taken a great deal of time and trouble in his methods of communication. After a series of hits and misses he had set up his connection and he was damned if he'd let it be used as a party-line.

"Sorry," Jack mumbled sadly, and withdrew his face from the pan. He could enjoy it vacariously, he consoled himself. But Joseph, knowing he was listening in put an end to the day's session. "Tomorrow, Madalena," he shouted.

"What about the hips, the hips, the hips?" Madalena was far from exhausted.

"I'll have your hips," Jack shouted into the pan.

"Get off my line, you bastard," Joseph said. "Don't talk, Madalena. Please." The thought of Madalena being taken from under his nose by a suitor who was equally anonymous was unbearable. "You're not for him, Madalena."

"Joseph, Joseph," she said, making her choice clear. "Tomorrow, Joseph," she said.

There were sounds of cross kisses through the bends, and Jack threw in a couple for good measure. He wasn't going to lick the steam off anyone's windows. Tomorrow he'd go right in.

He leaned his head against the pan. For some reason he felt ashamed, like one who gatecrashes, not out of bravado, but desperation. He had crouched like an animal at a foreign lair, an uninvited third party, and he shivered with the humiliation of it all.

Ruth went to the Consulate every day, and every day the matter had passed into different if not higher hands. Yes, they were doing their best. They had no doubt that the outcome of their efforts would be satisfactory. In view of the offender's nationality and tourist status, the court was not unwilling to review his case, but these things take time, Mrs Millar, and no little diplomacy.

On the sixth day, Ruth left the Consulate, desolate, lonely and not knowing what to do. She followed the streets for miles; the shops disappeared and the houses were scattered without neighbours. Then a sudden familiarity with the landscape excited her, and she heard the distant singing of the sea. She ran towards the sound, not stopping until the white waves fairly broke upon her forehead. She sank down on the sands and there it was still, like a great black wart on the shore's face, the seal, stubbornly forbidding burial. She knelt down on the wet caked sand of the vault, and resting her hand on the black shining hump, for the first time since Jack had been taken she let herself cry aloud. The foetid smell of the hump did not disturb her; she sobbed gratefully on to the smooth oily back, her sobs drowned in the gulps of the ebbing tide.

## 23

As each day passed, Jack tried more and more to convince himself that putting his jigsaw together was pointless. Not only pointless, but dangerous too. It was enough to have collected the pieces. The seal, the old woman, Ruth, his mother, and all the motley periphery, were separate, clear and defined in his thinking, posed in his mind like puppets for the ultimate move in a cartoon. He didn't want to gel his jigsaw. He had collected and that was enough. To assemble it would be an act of dying, an orgasm of suicide.

His reasoning pleased him, but it made him restless too. He could now see little point in his continued imprisonment. He did not need solitude any more. He was ready to leave prison. He began to blame Ruth for failing in her mission. He had to find fault with her to offset his desperate longing to be with her. He looked forward to the exercise period and the silent company of other men.

The warder would be coming soon. He could tell from the sound of dribbling feet of the men who had already been called. The warder would come into his cell, put an arm round Jack's shoulder and usher him into the passing line on its way to the yard. Once among the men, the warder would have to drop his hand and Jack could straighten his shoulders and breathe deeply at the fresh air.

They ambled round in a circle. He was always behind

the same man who walked slowly, with an anonymous shuffle, his gait a grudged concession to the enforced parade. He had obviously done the yard-turn hundreds of times. You could always pick out the old timers. They took the fresh air with little appetite. Fresh air had become to them a chore. The silent company of men only increased their frustration. It was better in a stuffy cell, where talk was allowed with your cell-mates in whom time had sieved all incompatability.

There was nothing recognizable in the man in front of him, except the scar at the back of his neck, probably the remains of an old carbuncle. Jack walked erect, jutting out his chin on the turn of the circle so that the man behind him should know and remember him. He felt the man's pace quicken behind him and a voice whispered between his shoulder-blades, "Be with you next week," it said. Jack knew that in a few days he was to be moved and word had got round as to his change of address. He desperately wanted to turn round and look at the man with whom he was to share accommodation, but even on the turn of the line it was impossible because the man was so close behind him. He tried on the third turn but the man dogged him closely as if he wanted to keep himself as a surprise. On the tenth turn, which was the end of the day's ration, the line filtered into the dark corridors of the prison. The men slowed down adjusting their sights to the sudden change of light. The warder was at the end of the line, and it was an opportunity for Jack to turn around and examine his promised bed-fellow.

He was a tiny man, and Jack had to look down at him. His small eyes were buried under two untidy sprouts of grey eyebrow and his soft aimless nose wandered lazily at no angle in particular. But his lips, especially the lower one, protruded almost tangent to his nostrils. They were dry and cracked; he looked like an otter deprived of water for a long time. He looked round furtively to ascertain that the coast was clear, then he beckoned Jack with his lower lip.

"I've got a jigsaw," he whispered. "Six thousand pieces. You must help me. I've done it all but the middle. Only got another two years." He looked round once again. "A model railway," he added, smiling at the recollection.

He suddenly withdrew his lower lip, as if shutting his conversation-shop. Jack saw his warder coming down the line. He waited to receive the hand on his shoulder. He would have to endure it for at least twelve paces. Jack had become obsessed by the man's touch. He waited for it every morning before and after exercise and every time a meal was brought. He knew that it was a touch that he would remember all his life. He felt that his shoulder would forever bear the imprint of the man's hand, like a permanent weal.

He rushed into his room for the day's instalment of Madalena. He had not forgotten the shame he had felt at his last audience, but he promised himself that after today, he wouldn't tune in any more. He sat on his bunk, with one foot forward, at the ready to sprint to the pan. He heard the crackling warm-up of Joseph's wave-length, and swiftly he moved into position. "Madalena", he sang into the bowl.

"Get off my line," Joseph pleaded.

Jack was so moved by the urgency in his voice – Joseph had obviously been incarcerated longer than he – that he decided to settle in as a listener. Nobody could object to that. He pulled his head out of the pan and sat comfortably beside it. The day's conversation started off with Madalena's hips, but got no further than her thighs. Joseph was apparently starving, and soon exhausted. When they rang off with their cross-kisses, Jack was bitterly disappointed. But tomorrow, he consoled himself, held promise of great discoveries.

Early next morning the warder brought him news of his release. The Consulate had intervened on his behalf and he was to leave for England on the night plane. He doubted whether he could ever return to South Africa. He gave the news in a clipped official voice and when he had done he turned on his heel and left the cell. When he had gone Jack brushed his shoulder automatically. He was now convinced that the print would be there forever.

His first reaction to the news was one of disappointment. He would miss the day's instalment of Madalena. He wished he could postpone his release for another day. A picture of Madalena's thighs would be denied to him forever. He tried to imagine the half of herself that she had not revealed. He tried to patch on to her waist an imaginary body that suited the breasts she had so vividly described.

He toyed with lots of patterns; he even gave her a pair of white English legs, mottled with gas-fire, or varicose-veined like his mother's. At this last image he shivered and grabbed frantically at the clothes that the warder had returned to him.

When he had changed and was waiting for them to let him out, he once more looked around his cell. It was suddenly familiar and friendly. He thought of Ruth again, with eager but frightening anticipation. He knew by experience, how on seeing her, his excitement would wane, and persuaded himself that this time it must not be so. He dreaded their meeting. He wished he could have talked to Madalena just once more. He would have been more prepared to face his freedom. He went over to the lavatory pan to have one last stab at communication. He tapped on the inside of the enamel. "Testing. One, two, three, four." The line was dead. He thought enviously of the occupant who would follow him in his cell, who would eavesdrop for his diversion. Perhaps one day they would meet, and with their separate findings put Madalena together. But he too, his successor, would be a man who would leave love behind and who would ache and curse himself for company. This thought renewed his longing for Ruth, and compassion for the man who would inherit his cell. He wanted to leave something for him, some mark of understanding, some proof that he had been there, had survived the four white walls, and left. He remembered that a few days ago the warder had inadvertently dropped a piece of chalk on to his blanket. Jack had hidden it in his mattress. Now he clutched it in his hand and he looked around for somewhere in the cell on which he could make his mark. There was little choice of surfaces and he settled finally for the inside wall of the bucket. He didn't think of what message he would leave; he was concerned solely with transferring to the next tenant his sad but concrete sense of elation. He knelt down by the bucket and turned it on its side. He moistened the chalk with his tongue, stealing a nibble in the process, and without thinking, he wrote on the zinc surface, *"I love you"*.

Summer was steaming the Cape and the table-cloth mist lay daily over Table Mountain like seasonal manna. Ralph had been quite right and Priscilla had by now patted her head over to England. Jan was guiding suckers over the country, while Robert washed down the dirty walls. The seal still lay on Strandfontein beach, a stinking denial of burial, and the notice boards acknowledged the corpse, for the smell was right and proper. Over on the sand dune the beggar kissed or beat his toes according to his turnover.

In his prison cell Jack sat trembling, while in her hotel bedroom Ruth trembled too.

He was not due out until late afternoon, and it was still early morning. The luggage, his and hers, was piled ready at the door. The passports and the tickets for the night plane out of Cape Town were in her bag. There remained about seven hours to be lived through before the nightmare was over. She daren't think of their meeting at the prison gates. She didn't want in any way to calculate what she would say to him, or how she would look at him, if indeed she could look at him or say anything at all. She looked at herself in the mirror. She had been ready for hours. Her suit was neatly pressed, her stocking seams straight, a raised pile on her suede shoes and her face carefully and sparsely made up. Behind her ears his favourite scent and a small phial for refuelling was ready in her handbag. She was restless and wanted to hasten her departure. Only one finish-touch remained. She had not yet lacquered her hair. Once or twice she had laid her finger on the spray-button, but each time she had recollected Jack's withdrawing hand. She patted her hair into place and was reminded of Priscilla. The recollection of their ill-omened meeting horrified her, and she picked up the bottle decisively. Holding it above her head she pressed on the button until the spray was exhausted. She hurried out of the room to arrange for a taxi to pick up the luggage and to settle her bill.

She decided to start walking towards the prison. She was too restless to wait in her room. She wanted to greet Jack with flowers and she made for the flower market in the centre of the town. She went from stall to stall examining the blooms.

She finally settled on a single protea in full flower. They would take it to England, where, over a period of several months, it would blacken into death. She could no longer wait to be with Jack and she walked quickly to the precincts of the prison. She stood at the gate, her eyes fixed on the entrance. In one hand she held the protea and with the other she smoothed her lacquered hair. The feel of it sickened her as she realized that she had wanted to punish him. She turned and ran back to the flower-market. There in the centre was a gushing fountain. She bent forward, spraying her hair against the main jet. A small crowd gathered to stare at her, grew bored, and went about their business. When she had finished, she hurried back to the prison, and brushed her hair dry under the blazing sun.

Jack knew that outside the wall, Ruth was waiting for him. He was bursting with love for her, with remorse, and with all kinds of ideas of recompensing her for all she had suffered on his behalf. He wondered what she was wearing outside the wall. He tried to comb her wardrobe but all was blurred. Only her long black hair he remembered. It seemed already to be touching him.

In the late afternoon, when the cell bolts were drawn on the men inside, they came together at the gates of the prison. They kissed wordlessly, crushing the protea between them. With his head over her shoulder, he gathered her loose hair into a bun. "I love her," he said to himself, and he hoped to God that he would be able.

# 24

They waited in the lounge of the airport. It was barely a fortnight since they had landed in Cape Town and three-quarters of the time Jack had spent in prison. He was glad they were leaving and he was restless for the plane to take off. He saw the lobby door swing open and a man, half-familiar, strode with sad and stubborn purpose directly towards him. It was Paul, and Jack nudged Ruth as he approached them. He stopped opposite Jack looking down at him, and without any greeting he said, "I know it wasn't *you.*"

"What wasn't me?"

"It wasn't you. It couldn't have been. You were in prison." He was suddenly agitated, and Ruth was moved by his distress.

"Sit down, Paul," she said. "How is Vicki?" For some reason she regretted having asked.

"I thought perhaps you didn't know," Paul said, almost to himself.

"Know? Know what?" Though Ruth and Jack felt they knew already.

"She's dead."

Ruth shuddered. No-one she knew had seemed more indestructible than Vicki, but what saddened her most was not Vicki's death, but the picture of Paul so bereft, who had so obviously loved her, and who could put up with her no longer.

"She's dead, my Vicki," Paul whispered.

Ruth felt she ought to ask how it happened, but she feared it would sound chatty, and in any case the cause of Vicky's death was quite irrelevant. "How are you managing?" she asked instead.

"I survive," he said. "Although we expected it, it was still a shock when it came.

"We? Did she know?" Jack asked.

"She'd known for six months. But she never told me. The doctor called me one day and he told me, but I never let her know that I knew. It was an unknown and unshared secret between us. It was difficult at times. I wanted to give her so much and I was afraid she'd get suspicious." He put his hand to his eyes, shutting out the almost-given present, the extra embrace with-held. "She started to buy chrysanthemums," he went on, a tiny smile on his face, "and they were delivered to the house in cart-loads. Whenever I asked her, 'Why chrysanthemums, why *only* chrysanthemums', she used to laugh and say 'They smell like the earth'." Paul lowered his head. "I suppose she wanted to get used to the smell," he said.

Ruth shivered. His cold logic horrified her, yet it seemed to give him strength.

"That's why she always dressed as a bishop at the parties," he went on. "She'd never go as a pawn or even royalty. 'I'm sticking to the church,' she used to say." He giggled shyly. "I suppose she wanted to get on the right side of things before she went.'

Ruth put her hand on his arm and he tried to suppress his giggling. He was surviving by the comedy of it all, trying to mask the deep love he felt for her.

Ruth sensed his need to talk about it. "Tell me about it," she said.

Paul stared across the tarmac. "It happened after a chess party," he said. "Only a week ago. Towards the end we used to give one of those parties every night. It was one long nightmare of bishops and chrysanthemums. It was after one of those parties, in the morning. I'd gone to bed halfway through the night and in the morning I went downstairs to have breakfast with Vicki. I found her on the floor in the dining-room, sprawled over the chess-board from rook to pawn." He looked back at Ruth and Jack as if still puzzled by his discovery. He took Ruth's hand and squeezed it. "I'll never know who shared her last hours," he whispered. "I'll never know who cheated me of her dying. All I know is that it wasn't you," he put his hand on Jack's arm. "You have a fool-proof alibi."

Paul was crying. He tried to go on with his story but he had to pause to collect himself. "I had waited six months to share her final love, and it was stolen from me." The horror of the theft seemed to incense him, and he raised his voice. "Some masked monster lay by her side and poured poison into her," he shouted.

Ruth squeezed his arm. "But at least she died in harness, my Vicki," he smiled, "even if it was death itself who slept with her." Suddenly he gripped Jack's arm. "But who did she confess to?" he asked earnestly. "It nags at me, and how shall I ever know? I walk in the street and I see men who, beneath their hoods or masks all look the same. And I know that among them there is one whose face is sprayed with my Vicki's last breath. She was mine," he screamed, "I loved her and I shared her, but only I had the right to deliver her."

He got up slowly without looking at them and blindly

groped his way past the chairs. They watched him as he disappeared through the door, his head bowed and his mind a frantic sorting-house of hoods and masks.

Ruth took Jack's arm and they walked together to the waiting plane without once looking behind them.

On the way home, as he slept, Jack had a dream. He stood fishing by the water at Cape Point and out of the Indian Ocean came Madalena, swimming round the bend. First her nipples, then her breasts, followed by her hips and thighs. Afterwards there was no more. From the Atlantic side Joseph was swimming towards her, and when they reached each other he picked up the black amputee and took her far out into the ocean. Jack cast his fishing-rod in their direction.

"Get on my line," he pleaded, "get on my line."

"It wasn't you," Joseph shouted back at him. "I know it wasn't you."

# 25

After two months in England, it was as if nothing had happened. Jack had vague recollections of an abrupt nightmare, and he went daily to his work with the aftertaste of waking. At times, at his desk, he tried to recollect the experience, to see himself as having played a part in it. But all that had happened on their journey appeared so meaningless, that he could not even acknowledge that it had happened to him. Alone in his office, he loved Ruth with a deluge of resolutions to love her at home. But each night, he knew the horror of the vacuum between them. He needed a bridge to her, but he didn't want any more third parties. He had to build the bridge himself. You couldn't trust other builders. You never knew how reliable they were. Some would die, or work for someone else, or just didn't pay off at all. He had to build his own bridge to Ruth, reinforce what was faulty, and support what was weak. He had to know the nature of the hyphen between them as well as he knew himself. But how?

One morning, he gave Ruth a lift into town, and before going to his office, they had coffee together. He tried to avoid it. He had enough with the wordless breakfast and dinner sessions, and he couldn't imagine why she should wish to find other locations for their silences. But Ruth had a reason. Today was their second wedding anniversary, and over breakfast Jack had said nothing. She wanted to give him extra time to remember. Or perhaps he had not forgotten, and was also wondering why she had made no reference to it. Had neither of them forgotten, but had found it indecent to recall?

They went into a small café near his office. Jack ordered and they waited wordlessly. Ruth fiddled inside her handbag.

"What are you looking for?" he said.

"My diary. What date is it today?" she could not refrain from giving him a clue.

He thought for a moment. "The eighth," he said. He did not react at all, and Ruth knew he had forgotten.

She looked across at him and saw him smile in the direction of the doorway. She didn't want to look round, but she followed his smile until it settled obliquely past her. She turned and caught a fleeting glance of a girl sitting at a table just behind her, but directly into Jack's line of vision. Ruth felt herself doublecrossed by the girl's deliberate choice of table. She could hardly keep turning round to see what occasioned Jack's reaction. As the waitress brought their coffee, Ruth looked out of the window. A bus stopped outside and in its dark background the window became a mirror for the girl behind her. While the bus was waiting, Ruth examined the new customer. Even in the elongated reflection she threw on to the glass, the girl was very attractive. A boy's school-cap sat on her closely cropped head and a pair of plain gold sleepers pierced her small ears. In the window, she looked about nine years old. The bus moved off and erased the picture, and Ruth could not resist turning to verify the girl's age. About twenty, but with a child's soap-shiny innocence. She turned back to look at Jack, and felt badly-dressed and very old. If only he could give her some assurance. If only he understood that she needed it. 'Please don't ask for it,' she pleaded with herself. 'Don't ask him if you look nice. He'll say yes without looking.'

She caught Jack smiling at her. He took her hand. "Darling, you should buy a new coat," he said. "Why don't you get one this morning? Let me give you a cheque," he said, feeling in his wallet.

She had heard it before. Buy yourself something. Here's thirty pounds worth of my conscience to be getting on with. Put it on your back.

"Buy yourself something," he said. "You haven't bought anything for yourself since we came back."

She saw him smile at the girl again, as he looked up from signing the cheque. She took it from him. "Thanks." If only he had remembered the anniversary, it would have been a valid present. She couldn't have seen through it so easily.

Another bus pulled up at the stop, and a wide screen settled on to the window-frame. She saw the girl nodding in Jack's direction. Unmistakably. She looked quickly at Jack to see what the girl was agreeing to. She saw the end of a word on his lips and a cadence of a gesture in his hand. She wanted to get out quickly. She had seen and been it all before.

"Would you like some more coffee?" Jack asked.

Why should she prolong the encounter for him? The bus was still waiting but she didn't want to look any more. It would have been like reading his letters.

"I want to go," she said.

"What's the matter?"

"It's stuffy in here. In any case, I want to get to the shops before they're too crowded." Why did she have to lie just in order to protect him, as he had to lie to protect her?

She clutched at his hand. "Let's be honest with each other, Jack," she pleaded.

"Why, what's the matter."

What's the matter, for God's sake. Two years married and forgotten, half of it vicariously to his mother and Miss Rallim, the other half neglected, and every minute of it alone, and what's the matter, for God's sake.

"Nothing."

Normally he would have shouted at her. But the terrifying lightheartedness was creeping on him already. "Let's get into the air," he said.

He paid the bill and directed her out of the café, taking care to walk behind her. Outside he put his arm around her shoulder. "We ought to go out a bit more," he said. "Shall I take you out to dinner, tonight?" His tone of abandon pierced her. She was positive now that he had forgotten the anniversary. Remembering would have made everything so much easier. It would have blunted the lie a little. It would have made her feigned belief in him believable.

"Yes," she said. "I'd love to eat out. I'll buy a new coat."

She was not surprised that he kissed her on leaving. Nor did it surprise her that he told her he loved her. She walked away trembling. At the corner she leaned against the wall to steady herself. She looked back in the direction of the café, and was just in time to see Jack disappearing into the door.


As she entered the house the phone was ringing. As she expected. It would be Jack. He had to take a client out to dinner. The monotony of the pattern wearied her. She doubted whether she could go through it all again. Yet she knew she would, again and again; human endurance was offensively inexhaustible. She picked up the phone wearily.

"Hello?"

The line crackled, and the voice on the other end, a woman's voice, was very indistinct. "Are you Payling 1944?"

"Yes," Ruth answered.

"I have a greetings telegram for Mr and Mrs Millar. Can you hear me? This line is terrible."

"Yes," Ruth said through the crackle.

"All our . . ." the rest of the sentence was drowned in the buzz on the line.

"I can't hear," Ruth shouted. She heard the panic in her voice. She needed the message whatever it was. It was important that somebody had remembered. "Can you repeat that?" she tried again. "Oh yes," Ruth echoed the operator, "all our wishes?"

The operator took over. "All our wishes for your . . ." Again the crackle intervened.

"For my what?" Ruth pleaded. "Can you spell it?" she said helplessly.

The line suddenly cleared and the operator's voice sang out loud and clear. "H-A-P-P-I—"

"Yes," she said. "Did it have as many as two 'p's and that many letters?"

"Love," the operator was still reading "Mompop. That's one word," she added, bewildered.

"Mompop," Ruth repeated. The one word had saved them a couple of pennies, but they hadn't economized on the 'love'. They had paid full price for that one. 'Mompop', she said to herself again, and somehow it seemed right that in their union they should have between them but

242

one name. "Ruthjack," she tried aloud. "Jackruth." It didn't work. It just didn't work at all. Jackmotherruth. Jackrallimruth, Jackanybodyruth, they all had a better rhythm, and such would be the tempo of her life forever.

She didn't mind crying when no one was there, except that it left her eyes red-ringed for hours. She would have to start the long accustomed practise of swabbing them with cold water. She rationed herself out a portion of tears and went to the bathroom to obliterate the traces. She sat on the stool facing the sink, and turned round to dab her eyes before the light. She caught sight of the door. A straight white panel of wood, unscratched, unscathed, unaccusable. She wondered why its unblemished whiteness offended her. Then she remembered her mother's bathroom, and the door which shut out on one side of it all the clamour of the Lazarus *angst*. The bathroom in her mother's house, and probably in most houses, she thought, was the only room which locked, the only room in which one could find a guaranteed privacy and refuge. In her mother's house, each member of the family had, at some time or another, donated a scar to the door. She herself, when very young, had half-heartedly threatened suicide, convinced that her parents were not her parents at all. She had run noisily to the bathroom, and even more noisily bolted the door. Poor Mrs Lazarus, with panic and ladle came running after her. "Ruth," she screamed. "Open the door." Ruth hadn't answered. She just stood behind the door and watched the reverberation of her mother's shrieks. "Open the door," Mrs Lazarus yelled, "or I'll kill you." She had rushed to the landing to call her husband. Ruth heard her father rushing up the stairs, and her mother screaming for him to hurry. Mr Lazarus had delivered one strong kick at the base of the door. Ruth was terrified when she saw his boot come through. The toe-cap had such an unmistakeably proletarian shine, it made her cry. Defeated, she had opened the door. A slab of new wood was eventually hammered across the base. But it was a splendid scar. It was made of love and attention. It made the door a better door, and the bathroom of better refuge. Even Grandma sought shelter in there to read letters that she wanted nobody to see. And her brothers had hidden there, from each other and their Hebrew lessons. The bolts had been continually replaced, and the locks re-fashioned. "Ruth loves Edwin," was engraved on one panel, and "I hate Grandma" on another. It was a door behind which people had privately succumbed or resisted to joy or sorrow. And the scars on the door told their history.

Now she knew why the whiteness of her own door offended her. In all her marriage, out of her despair and occasional joy, she had registered nothing, and neither, which was more frightening, had Jack. Were they so self-contained, those two, even in their privacy? She got up and took a nail file from the shelf. Leaning against the door she deflowered the white panel. "I AM HERE," she scratched along the top. It was at least a beginning.

She went downstairs and sat next to the phone, waiting for Jack's call. She picked it up immediately it began to ring. She heard a cough and a slight hesitation at the other end of the line.

"Hullo?" Hullo?" she said.

"Ruth? It's me. Are you back already? Just a minute. There's somebody on the other line."

"You phoned me," she said. "What's the point of doing it when you're busy? Ring me back when you're free," she said coldly. She replaced the receiver.

Her prompt answering had put him off his guard. He was playing for time. He was probably now rehearsing what he would say to her. He was probably writing it down on the pad in front of him. "I've got to take a client to dinner tonight. The one who just phoned. No, it's an awful bore. I don't know what time I'll be home. No, don't wait up for me."

Ruth sat down near the telephone. She felt weak. I can't go through it again, she thought. She determined that this time, she would make a stand. She began to rehearse what she would say to him. "What's the name of your client? I don't believe you. Where are you eating then? That's a man's club isn't it? Very clever. No, I don't believe a word. I won't wait up for you. I won't be here when you get back. I'm leaving right now." She hoped he would ring soon, before her determination left her.

The phone rang and she picked it up weakly. "Hullo?"

"Do you sit on that phone?" he laughed. "Did you buy a coat?"

"No. I couldn't find one."

"There must have been something. I'll come with you tomorrow, shall I? Look," he hurried on, "I can't take you out tonight, darling. A client's just called. I have to be with him."

"That's a pity," she said.

"We'll go out tomorrow," he said. "I may be late, darling."

"I won't wait up for you."

"We'll get a coat tomorrow, yes?"

"What's the date today?" she pleaded with him.

"You asked me before, darling," he laughed. "It's the eighth, or something. I'll see you later." He was

245

obviously anxious to ring off and she made it easy for him.

She let the day swallow itself unnoticeably. She found herself watching television until it was dark. The images were blurred and the sounds meaningless. Use our lipstick and Gary Cooper will marry you. Our hand cream will give your dog a longer life. Polish your floor with quick-look and your husband will sleep with you regular. Your neighbour's husband is regular and it shows. Your breath smells. Honey-sweet, liquid-soft. Life's tough and if you've got to go, go by gas. Interval after interval of empty promises, pauses for tea-making, recitatives. Our tea will make him regular too, and so will bird-feed, cat-crap, chap-sap, regular regular night-cap, and on and on and on until the queen rode out on a horse and was saved.

As she turned to go to her bed, she heard his key in the door. She heard the familiar tip-toe, and she knew there would be heartiness in his voice. "Still up?" he said, kissing her. "Let's go to bed." He followed her to the bedroom, shutting the door behind him. "Coat tomorrow?" he said. "And dinner?" He spoke as if he were addressing a child, with the same abandon that she remembered from Miss Rallim's days. Somewhere he had found another arsenal, and he had returned, equipped. Tonight, she would be served.

He undressed and was quickly in bed. "You forgot, didn't you?" he accused her, with a smile.

"I was waiting for you to remember. I was dropping hints all day."

"Why didn't you say so then? Come on to bed," he whispered. "We must celebrate."

The cheap monstrous lie of it all. She began to undress,

knowing she was committing herself to the uncommittable.

"Open another window, darling," he said. "It's stuffy in here."

She went to the bay and opened the window wide. And she wondered why there did not emerge from the linoed bed-sitters and the edge to edge rooms, over the great silent city, one vast discordant cry of pain.

# GO TELL THE LEMMING

## *Bernice Rubens*

'Dear Angela. I can't stand it any more, so I'm going to put my head in the gas oven . . .'

For Angela Morrow the death of her marriage is the ultimate in rejection. She debates whether to address her suicide note to her parents, to her son or to David, her defecting husband – and end up writing it to herself. In fact, Angela writes to Angela quite a lot.

But David, a successful film producer, is beginning to prefer Angela's unpredictability to the vacuous calm of his mistress. He invites her to work on location in his new film. So Angela postpones killing herself and goes instead to Rome . . .

·0 349 10147 7
ABACUS

# CLOSELY OBSERVED TRAINS

*Bohumil Hrabal*

For gauche young apprentice Milos Hrma, life at the small but strategic railway station in Bohemia in 1945 is full of complex preoccupations. There is the exacting business of dispatching German troop trains to and from the toppling Eastern front; the problem of ridding himself of his burdensome innocence; and the awesome scandal of Dispatcher Hubicka's gross misuse of the station's official stamps upon the telegraphist's anatomy. Beside these, Milos's part in the plan for the ammunition train seems a simple affair.

*Closely Observed Trains*, which became the award-winning Jiri Menael film of the 'Prague Spring', is a classic of postwar literature, a small masterpiece of humour, humanity and heroism which fully justifies Hrabal's reputation as one of the best Czech writers of today.

0 349 101256
ABACUS FICTION

# LOVING AND GIVING

## *Molly Keane*

In 1914, when Nicandra is eight, all is well in the big Irish house called Deer Forest. Maman is beautiful and adored. Dada, silent and small, mooches contentedly around the stables. Aunt Tossie, of the giant heart and bosom, is widowed but looks splendid in weeds. The butler, the groom, the land-steward, the maids, the men – each has a place and knows it. Then, astonishingly, the perfect surface is shattered; Maman does something too dreadful ever to be spoken of.

'What next? Who to love?' asks Nicandra. And through her growing up and marriage her answer is to swamp those around her with kindness – while gradually the geat house crumbles under a weight of manners and misunderstanding.

0 349 10088 8
**ABACUS FICTION**

# LOVE AND FRIENDSHIP

*Alison Lurie*

'The day on which Emily Stockwell Turner fell out of love with her husband began much like other days . . .' Love and Friendship is Alison Lurie's much acclaimed first novel. Rich, beautiful and innocent, Emily is shocked by her lack of feeling for her dependable husband, Holman, and appalled though intriqued, by the notion that she could fall in love outside marriage.

Set in a quiet New England university town which thrives on academic quarrels and gossip, Love and Friendship is a witty and forthright examination of the conventions and contradictions of love, sex and marriage.

'She writes with great elegance . . . very funny as well'
*Observer*

'A brilliant and seemingly effortless accomplishment'
*Sunday Telegraph*

0 349 122121
FICTION

# NO. 4 PICKLE STREET

## *David Peak*

This is Kate's story, the fiction of her life. Trapped in marriage
with a complacent fathead of a man, she starts writing a journal.
As she recalls her lost lover, J, she lives again the high erotic
charge of their relationship, and recreates the circumstances of
their passion – a room with an old mahogany bed, abandoned
Chinese takeaways, Tom Waits on the record player, games with
chocolate buttons, nakedness.

As she sifts through past and present, she finds the urge to colour
in her life with extravagant shades – to fantasise, build castles in
the air – too powerful to resist. Fact and fiction merge to reveal
the truth about Kate and the origins of her suffering.

0 349 10174 4
**ABACUS FICTION**

# THE WHITE CUTTER

## *David Pownall*

In the thirteenth century, an age half-crazed in its quest for certainty, King Henry seeks solace in the building of cathedrals. But Christians do not make good architects. To create the illusion of permanence – those soaring wonders in stone – Henry knows to rely on the masons, the secret brotherhood whose very craft disguises a dangerous heresy and creates a blasphemous beauty.

THE WHITE CUTTER is the confession of Hedric, son of an itinerant stonemason, reared in a tool-bag, who becomes the greatest architect of his age. It tells of rumbustious adventures; of his sexual apprenticeship; of his unique education; of rogue clerics, singular nuns and The Four, a secret cabal teetering on the brink of genius and dementia.

It is a book which reveals much about light and stone, God and the Devil, father and sons, the Church and the State, love and murder, our need for secrecy and our need for uncontradicted truth in an age of chaos.

0 349 10117 5
ABACUS FICTION

# THE QUIET WOMAN

*Christopher Priest*

Dread is seeping into the quiet world of Alice Hazeldine. The lead from a French nuclear reactor has poisoned the Wiltshire atmosphere; her latest book, an apparently innocuous biography of six women, has been inexplicably impounded by the Home Office. Now, shockingly, her intelligent elderly neighbour Eleanor Hamilton has been brutally murdered.

Why had Eleanor never mentioned the son who turns up for her funeral? Why was he censored from her past as surely as bureaucratic paranoia is censoring Alice's present? Uncannily, she find herself slipping into a vortex where the borderline between the real and the unreal, the mundane and the apocalyptic become disturbingly – and increasingly – confused . . .

0 349 10195 7
**ABACUS FICTION**

# THE BEAUTIFUL MRS SEIDENMAN

*Andrzej Szczypiorski*

The beautiful Jewish widow Irma Seidenman has three attributes
that keep her out of the Warsaw ghetto: a blonde hair, blue eyes,
and excellent forged papers. But one day in 1943 an informer
denounces her to the Gestapo – and in the thirty-six hours
following her arrest unlikely links are forged between a chain of
disparate people – Poles, Jews and Germans, with motives
righteous and base – in the attempt to rescue her.

Ranging back and forward in time, by turns tender, ironic, sad
and funny, Szczypiorski constructs a pattern of intersecting lives in
a masterly and deeply compassionate exposition, not just of
Warsaw, but of all victims, persecutors and spectators alike in a
world at war.

0 349 10094 2
ABACUS FICTION

| | | |
|---|---|---|
| ☐ Seton Edge | Bernice Rubens | £4.99 |
| ☐ Brothers | Bernice Rubens | £5.99 |
| ☐ Mr Wakefield's Crusade | Bernice Rubens | £4.99 |
| ☐ Our Father | Bernice Rubens | £4.99 |
| ☐ Birds of Passage | Bernice Rubens | £4.99 |
| ☐ Sunday Best | Bernice Rubens | £4.99 |
| ☐ Ponsonby Post | Bernice Rubens | £4.99 |
| ☐ Elected Member | Bernice Rubens | £4.99 |
| ☐ Spring Sonata | Bernice Rubens | £4.99 |
| ☐ Five Year Sentence | Bernice Rubens | £4.99 |
| ☐ Madame Sousatzka | Bernice Rubens | £4.99 |

Abacus now offers an exciting range of quality titles by both established and new authors. All of the books in this series are available from:
Sphere Books, Cash Sales Department,
P.O. Box 11, Falmouth, Cornwall TR10 9EN

Alternatively you may fax your order to the above address. Fax No. 0326 76423.

Payments can be made as follows: Cheque, postal order (payable to Macdonald & Co (Publishers) Ltd) or by credit cards, Visa/Access. Do not send cash or currency, UK customers: please send a cheque or postal order (no currency) and allow 80p for postage and packing for the first book plus 20p for each additional book up to a maximum charge of £2.00.

B.F.P.O. customers please allow 80p for the first book plus 20p for each additional book.

Overseas customers including Ireland, please allow £1.50 for postage and packing for the first book, £1.00 for the second book, and 30p for each additional book.

NAME (Block Letters) ....................................................................

ADDRESS................................................................................

........................................................................................

☐ I enclose my remittance for _____

☐ I wish to pay by Access/Visa Card

Number ☐☐☐☐☐☐☐☐☐☐☐☐☐☐☐☐

Card Expiry Date ☐☐☐☐